STANDING DEAD

A Midcoast Maine Mystery

Also by Lawrence Rotch

Gravely Dead: A Midcoast Maine Mystery
Bulletproof: A Midcoast Maine Mystery

STANDING DEAD

A Midcoast Maine Mystery

Lawrence Rotch

S.P

Shoal Waters Press

Printed in the United States of America

ISBN 978-0-9839079-0-9

Library of Congress Control Number: 2011938806

First Edition: November 2011

Published by
Shoal Waters Press
Liberty, Maine
Shoalwaterspress.com

10 9 8 7 6 5 4 3 2 1

"The first thing a principle does is kill somebody."

Dorathy L. Sayers, *Gaudy Night*

Chapter 1

Carl Mueller pulled to the side of the narrow road and parked his pickup as far off the pavement as he dared without landing in the ditch. He was thirty miles from the Maine coast as the crow flies and there were few houses here, just seemingly endless woods on all sides.

Carl had parked nearly a mile away from Derwin Denton's woodlot and he walked the distance briskly, barely raising a sweat in the cool, dry morning air.

Carl checked for any passing cars before he slipped around one of Denton's No Trespassing signs, and moved into the woods. Safely out of sight, he pulled out his handheld GPS and began to walk a methodical search pattern through the woodlot. The property had a mile of frontage on the road, and extended two miles back into empty woodland, so there was a lot of ground to cover.

Carl walked roughly parallel to the road, zig-zagging back and forth as he worked his way from the front of the property towards the back.

The cool mid-September air, absence of mosquitos, deer flies, and other insect annoyances made for an ideal day to hike in the woods. Carl was in his forties, blond, tanned, and athletic, someone who could comfortably cover fifteen miles in a day—which was what he planned to do.

September not only signaled the end of summer, but the end of Derwin Denton's woodlot as well. Even now, Carl could hear the sound of distant chainsaws—Jack Fournier and his crew, cutting on the neighboring lot a couple of miles up the road.

He pushed his way through a section of overgrown brush and young trees, moving ever deeper into the woods as he watched the GPS unit in his hand. He guessed that the area where he was standing had been cut over within the last ten years. Most of the trees were small, little more than saplings, and the young undergrowth made it impossible to see more than a few dozen yards.

———

As luck would have it, Carl's truck, with its "SOCC" logo on the door, was spotted almost immediately.

The stalker knew what Carl was up to, which made it easy to prepare a suitable reception.

———

A sudden crashing sound nearby made Carl jump—just a deer, browsing on the small trees and brush, and startled by Carl's approach. He'd spent much of his life hiking in the woods, but today he felt strangely uneasy, the brush closing in on him, hiding unknown dangers.

Clambering up a rocky ledge, he suddenly found himself in a stand of huge, old-growth pines. The brush had long since been shaded out by the towering trees, leaving the space open, the ground soft with pine needles. The air was hushed and still, as though the great, silent trees had absorbed all of the life force from the air and taken it to themselves.

The heavy quietness of the place felt like the inside of an ancient church, with its feel of timelessness and unseen power.

No, not a church, Carl decided, moving on. He hurried his pace.

A little further into the pine woods, he was jolted by a place where the forest floor had been torn and slashed to mud by an ATV trail. Kids, probably. He wondered how old man Denton would feel about having his woodlot torn up by joyriders, though it would look a lot worse when the place was cut over.

He checked the GPS, changed course a bit, and found himself moving into thick, brushy woods again. A squirrel shot up a Spruce tree next to him, scolding as it went.

Carl had worked his way about half a mile in from the paved road, having covered some three miles of back-and-forthing, when he found what he was looking for: cedars, Northern White Cedars, Thuja Occidentalis, to be exact.

It was a small stand of trees, an acre or so, in a patch of boggy ground. Most of the trees were small, but there were three remarkably big specimens for Maine, though nothing like the giant Red Cedars on the west coast.

Different people find beauty and inspiration in different places. For some, it might be the loveliness of a woman, the sleek lines of a sports car, the magnificence of a piece of music, the radiance of a painting. For Carl it was the glory of a cedar tree. This was why he loved his work, and why he was here.

At their bases, the trunks bore the marks of blue spray paint—a forester's death sentence.

He gazed up at the mature trees, entranced by their clean, sweeping trunks, their velvety bark, their sprays of foliage reaching up to the sky, a delicate tracery of green on blue. He craned his neck, trying to see the top of the biggest cedar, but it was lost above the canopy. He stepped back, trying to get a glimpse, and discovered with a shock that the top had broken off.

"You do know this land is posted."

The voice behind him nearly made Carl jump out of his skin. "It is?" he replied blandly.

The stranger shrugged. "So, now you've found the stand of cedar."

"I'd heard about it anyway," Carl replied.

"And you're going to spend the whole day tramping around looking for more cedars?"

"That's what we do at SOCC," Carl said.

"Bunch of damn fools. I'd call the cops if there was cell phone coverage out here." The stranger shrugged again. "You looked up ahead, near the property line? I'll save you some walking, so you don't spend all day trespassing."

Carl followed his companion across the remains of an overgrown tote road and through a patch of thick woods until they suddenly came out to a place where a great slab of ledge lay just below the surface, making a natural clearing where only stunted trees and brush could clung to the thin soil.

"Take a look at this," the man said walking a few yards into the clearing to where a large tree, the only one that had managed to reach any size on the mossy, rocky ground, stood alone.

"It's an old beech tree," Carl said, wondering what this had to do with cedars. "The bark is diseased," he added noting the rough, wart-like surface. Carl looked up. "That's probably what killed it, that and the bad soil. Been dead for years."

"Look at those roots, spread out all over, right on the surface. Hard to see how a tree can stay standing without any soil to speak of."

"Are you suggesting that SOCC doesn't have a leg to stand on?" Carl said, as he studied the gnarled, twisted roots, which looked as though they were desperately trying to burrow into the ledge. "Why should I care about a standing dead beech—"

The blow caught Carl on the back of his head, driving him to the ground.

Carl could remember walking through the woods, the cathedral stillness of the big old pines, but why was he lying here? He tried to rise, but waves of pain and nausea forced him down.

He rested for a while, feeling the cool ground against his cheek, trying to grasp what had happened, waiting for the dizziness to pass, listening to the distant chain saws.

The trouble was, they didn't sound all that far away. Where was he? How long had he been here? Panic seized him.

Overhead, the dead beech swayed slightly, as though cringing from the saw's bite. Slowly, reluctantly, it began to lean.

Carl's world drifted in and out of focus as he fought for consciousness, trying to crawl across the ledge like a crippled bug.

The tree was tilting farther now, hinging on the remaining narrow strip of wood. While Carl crawled in slow motion, the tree leaned faster and faster until it crashed with a thud that shook the rocky ground.

Chapter 2 _____

The old woman knelt amidst a forest of tomato vines, filling her basket with the ripest specimens.

"I always put in too many plants each the spring," she said. Kate Merlew was in her eighties, with her white hair tied in a bun, and the frail, uncertain look of one who is struggling with chronic disease. "It's a good thing you like tomatoes," she added to her companion.

Sarah Cassidy, nearly thirty years younger, her brunette, shoulder-length hair touched with gray, her face as Irish as her name, knelt beside Kate. "I like the flavor of these."

"They are good, aren't they?" Kate replied. "I always had this variety when we lived in Massachusetts, and we liked them, so I plant them here, too. The trouble is, they aren't a short-season variety, so they don't always ripen before the frost hits."

"A lot of them are red already, though," Sarah said, glancing at Kate's basket.

"I'm hoping we'll have another week or so before the first frost," Kate said as she reached into the vines to extract another tomato. "With luck, most of them will be ripe enough to pick by then."

"And there's always fried green tomatoes."

"One of the good things about fall." Kate agreed, rising painfully to her feet. "How about coming in and having a cup of tea?"

The vegetable garden was situated behind the Merlews' 1840's vintage Colonial, which in turn was located in the town of Burnt Cove in Midcoast Maine.

Kate led the way to the woodshed's back door, and through the woodshed into the kitchen.

At the far end of the woodshed from the house was attached a small, two-room apartment where Kate's mother had lived years ago, and where Sarah had been staying for the summer.

At Kate's invitation, Sarah had arrived in May, intending to spend a peaceful summer out in her little sixteen-foot sailboat—an elderly Herreshoff 12, whose comfortable seats and ample keel gave it the reassuring feel of a much larger boat. The plan had been to spend the time rethinking her life after her recent divorce, but the summer ended up providing a lot more excitement than she'd expected—and also more attachments.

Kate put water on for tea, sat across the worn, wood-topped kitchen table, and gazed at Sarah.

"How's Oliver this morning?" Kate asked.

"How did you know I was there?"

"A wood shaving in your hair. I figured you must have been up there helping him build his boat." Kate leaned over and removed the delicate curl of wood, rubbed it between her fingers. "Mmm, smells like cedar."

"It's really Oliver's father's client's boat, but it actually has a name now, *Daisy.*"

"*Daisy,* as in, 'Daisy, Daisy, Give me your answer do. I'm half crazy, All for the love of you?'"

"Maybe, though I'm not sure the owner is old enough to remember the song," Sarah commented.

"Not many people are, dear."

The tea kettle began to whistle, and Kate busied herself with the tea pot.

"You know Sam and I loved having you spend the summer with us," Kate said, as she set out cups and saucers. "It's always a treat to see one of our campers all grown up."

The Merlews had run a girl's camp, which Sarah had attended in her teens, some forty years ago.

Kate sat down, looking faintly embarrassed. "We don't want you to think we're chasing you out, but we did promise Sam's sister that she could spent the winter with us, starting next month. "What with her being widowed now, we're the closest family she has left." Kate had told Sarah all this back in May.

Sarah reached across the table and took Kate's hand. "I can't tell you how much I've appreciated having you let me stay here, but I have to go back to Sudbury soon anyway."

"People will miss you around here."

"Yes," Sarah replied, thinking about Oliver, as Kate undoubtably was as well. She released Kate's hand. "The trouble is, the Realtor down there wants to stage the house, so I have to get back, make arrangements, and keep an eye on what they're doing."

Kate watched Sarah's face, waiting for more.

"At least for a while," Sarah added, thinking again about Oliver.

"Will you be able to live in the house while people are wandering through it?"

"That's part of what I want to talk to the Realtor about. I should be able to get back here next month for a visit as soon as things are more settled down there."

"There are lots of places you could rent in town for the winter," Kate said commented, as her fingers toyed absentmindedly with the shaving.

Sarah watched Kate with the scrap of wood. It was more than

just selling the house, of course. Sarah had been divorced for barely seven months now, and she'd planned to spend the summer free of entanglements. Much had happened to derail those plans, and she still hadn't sorted out her feelings well enough to share them with Kate, or anyone else, for that matter.

"Of course you're welcome to come back and spend next summer with us," Kate said. There was a wistfulness in Kate's voice, as though she wasn't sure there would be a next summer for her.

Sarah involuntarily glanced at the shelf lined with pill bottles and tried to imagine how Sam would cope without Kate. They had always seemed like one person in all the years she had known them.

"We'll see how things go," Sarah replied.

Thanks to an anonymous benefactor, the headquarters of the Save Our Cedars Coalition, or SOCC, as it was known, had graduated from the kitchen table in Carl Mueller's bachelor pad to a cramped, run-down storefront in Augusta. Being the state capital, Augusta provided easy access to various forms of officialdom and conservation organizations, not to mention lawyers—a few of whom were willing to work pro bono.

As the name suggested, the organization's avowed, if quixotic, goal was save the cedar trees of Maine from over-cutting, preferably by legal means, though a bit of picketing was sometimes used as a tactic.

The group counted perhaps a dozen hard-core members, and another half-dozen or so who could be relied on to turn out for a rally, provided the weather was good and coffee and donuts were made available.

Martha Kirkland put down the phone and turned to her two companions, who were hand-lettering placards at a folding table.

"The police just got an anonymous tip," Martha said in a shaky voice. She was middle-aged, with short curly brunette hair and a solid, muscular build.

Martha was not a person who's voice became shaky often.

"What was it?" one of the placard workers asked, looking concerned.

Martha sat abruptly. "They wouldn't say, except that it narrows the search area, and they hope to find him soon."

"Somewhere in that big woodlot in Tyler?"

"That's where his truck was found," Martha replied dully.

The second placard maker put down her felt-tip pen and used her ink-stained fingers to sweep back a strand of long, blond hair. "I didn't think we were going to bother with that woodlot. We only know about one small stand of cedars in there."

Martha bristled at the implied criticism. "That's what Carl went to find out—to see if there are more cedars. Besides, if there are *any* cedars being harvested improperly, it's our duty to protect them."

The first placard maker finished her work of art and set it aside. "Do you suppose he got lost in the woods?"

"For more than a day?" the second placard maker said. "Not a chance, especially with his GPS. Something has happened to him, for sure."

All Martha could think of was the phrase "anonymous tip." The sense of dread that she felt from the phone call, grew.

The first placard maker frowned at her fellow artist. "The Warden's Service is running the search, so I'm sure they'll find him soon," she said soothingly.

"I just hope he's not lying in the woods somewhere, hurt," the second placard maker said.

"I'm going up to help them look for him," Martha announced determinedly.

The two placard makers glanced at each other. "I think it would be better to stay here and finish these," one of them replied. "We'd just be in the way up there."

Her words fell on deaf ears, for Martha was already on her way out the door.

Chapter 3 _____

Sarah Cassidy lay in bed staring up at the unfamiliar pattern of cracks which spider-webbed the ceiling, and wondering what she was doing here.

A strip of dawn sunlight that had eluded the drawn blinds only served to amplify the question.

The first answer was simple: she'd been helping Oliver Wendell build "his" boat, as Kate put it, and they had spent yesterday laying fiberglass cloth over the inverted hull and coating it with epoxy. It was one of those non-stop, all-day jobs, so they'd put together a late supper, and one thing had led to another—

The second answer was harder. She had known Oliver for all of five months. True, they had been hectic months, which made them more intense, but how well did she really know this man? She had jumped impetuously into her first marriage, which had ended in disaster. Had she thoughtlessly climbed onto another runaway train as it hurtled down the track to God knew where?

Sarah looked at Oliver's back as he lay on his side next to her. He was snoring gently, one foot sticking out from under the covers. Seen from close-up, his curly blond hair showed streaks of gray. They weren't visible from a distance, unlike the telltale strands in her brunette hair.

"I'm not moving in with you, Oliver," she said.

Oliver gave a startled snort and rolled over onto his back. "What?" he said groggily.

"I'm not moving in with you," she repeated.

"Okay," he replied, eying her cautiously.

"I only came to Maine for the summer, and it's September already."

"Umm."

"This was supposed to be a nice, peaceful summer in Maine where I could sort things out." She frowned at Oliver. "Without distractions."

"Umm." He ran his fingers down her arm.

Sarah gave him a dark look. "We've talked about this before. I've got to go back to Massachusetts, to Sudbury, and figure out what to do with my house. The Realtor hasn't even gotten a nibble on the place, and I can't leave it empty all winter."

"Umm."

"Is 'umm' all you can say?" she demanded.

"You can't stay on with the Merlews?"

"I can't mooch off them forever—they won't let me pay them anything for using their granny flat and the heating season is beginning. Besides, Sam's sister will be staying there." She glanced at her watch. "God, look at the time. I'd better call them before they start worrying—"

Wes, Oliver's black-and-white Springer Spaniel, hopped onto the bed, insinuated himself between Sarah and Oliver, and flopped down with a contented sigh.

"Does he do this every morning?" she said.

"He heard you talking."

"I'm glad somebody did," she commented.

Just then, Wes exploded into a series of earsplitting barks and leapt off the bed.

"Ooof! Dammit, dog!" Sarah exclaimed.

"Somebody just drove up," Oliver said.

"Oh, hell," Sarah moaned.

Oliver got out of bed and kneeled down to peek under one of the blinds. He was naked, and she admired his back, noting a collection of freshly healed scars.

"It's Pearly," Oliver said. Parlin Gaites, or Pearly to his friends, was a local boatbuilder, somewhere on the far side of sixty-five years in age, who often dropped by to offer advice, help, and occasionally caustic remarks.

"I'll never live this down," Sarah muttered, clambering out of bed. She removed Oliver's oversized T-shirt and began to dress hurriedly.

Wes, the only one in the room who was truly enjoying Pearly's arrival, barked, wagged, and pirouetted with excitement.

"You still in bed at this hour?" Pearly bellowed from below the window.

"This is all your fault, Wendell," Sarah grumbled.

"Go the hell away," Oliver yelled down to Pearly.

"I'll go see how you're doing on that boat while you get dressed," Pearly replied. "Sounds like I'd better come in and make some coffee, too. Enough for three?" he added innocently.

———

Pearly sipped his coffee patiently while Sarah and Oliver ate. He looked around the kitchen, saying, "You've tidied up some. It usually looks like a pigsty in here."

"You don't like my housekeeping, stay out of my house," Oliver grumbled.

Sarah felt herself blush. She had cleaned up some of the kitchen mess yesterday while they were putting together supper—an impromptu omelet with some added onion, tomato, and bacon scrounged from the fridge. "He doesn't do too badly for a bachelor," Sarah commented.

Pearly looked at her for a moment as though about to say something, appeared to change his mind, and turned to Oliver. "You almost done sloshing sticky shit on that boat?" he inquired.

It wasn't that Pearly never used epoxy when he thought the situation demanded it—which wasn't often—it was just that he preferred the traditional ways, unlike Oliver who used modern techniques to build boats in wood. It was a cause for good-natured verbal sparring between the two.

"We need to sand it down, level out the hollows and bumps, and she'll be ready to roll over," Oliver replied, ignoring Pearly's jab.

Sarah frowned at the "we." What kind of assumptions was he making?

"Let me know when you're ready to turn her right side up," Pearly said. Oliver had planked the boat upside down since it was easier to work that way. It would have to be turned over to finish the inside.

"Eldon and I can come up," Pearly went on, "lend a hand, and make sure you don't drop the thing." Eldon Tupper happened to be in his mid-twenties, stood six-foot-six, weighed a muscular 300 pounds, and was immensely useful when it come to moving heavy objects.

"I'll count on it."

Pearly took a long swallow of coffee. "You remember the deal we have for that cedar, where you were going to saw it into boards for me?" Oliver had a small sawmill and often cut custom boat lumber for Pearly.

"I haven't seen the logs yet," Oliver replied.

"The deal has gotten complicated."

"Your deals always get complicated."

"Life gets complicated," Pearly said. "Problem is, the cedar is half a mile back in the woods and there's no tote road in there."

"So your logger makes one," Oliver said.

"Two problems with that—"

"I thought you said 'a' problem," Oliver replied.

"Stop interrupting. The first problem is that Jack Fournier, who's crew is going to cut the cedar, thought they were going to cut the whole woodlot—"

"And they're not?"

"You've met Jack and his crew," Pearly said. "They're small-time operators, and Denton's woodlot covers two square miles. It would take them forever to cut off the whole thing, and Denton doesn't want to wait that long, so he has a bigger crew lined up to cut the rest. Anyhow, Jack won't put the time and money into making a road just for a half-load of cedar, especially when somebody else will get to use the road for free to cut the rest of the land."

"Surely they can come to some kind of agreement," Sarah said.

Pearly shook his head. "You haven't met those guys. Getting them to agree on something would be like getting a pair of bulls to do the polka on a hockey rink. Bruce Nash—he's the other logger—is threatening to put his tote road on the far side of the property just to spite Jack."

"So have this Bruce Nash character cut your cedar, too," Oliver said.

Pearly took another swallow of coffee. "Can't do that because old Derwin Denton, who owns the woodlot, promised the job to Jack."

"So there's a third bull on the hockey rink?" Sarah said.

"You said two problems. What's the other one?" Oliver said suspiciously.

"Not a big problem, really. You remember Ralph, works on Jack's crew?"

"Ralph?" Oliver said. Looking out the kitchen window, he could see Wes inspecting the tires on Pearly's rusty Mazda pickup.

"One of Jack Fournier's wood cutting crew," Pearly prompted. "The old guy."

Oliver's mind conjured up Ralph: large, bald, in his seventies—a man who'd spent a lifetime working in the woods and looked it. "Yeah. What about him?"

"The cops think he murdered somebody," Pearly said, watching Oliver's reaction.

"Didn't seem like the killer type to me," Oliver commented, "though he doesn't care much for bureaucrats, as I remember. Especially Maine Forest Service types."

"Ralph wouldn't hurt a fly," Pearly said emphatically.

"Who was killed?" Sarah inquired.

"Guy named Carl Mueller. He runs a conservation group called SOCC."

"Sock?" Sarah said.

"Save Our Cedars Coalition," Pearly replied. "SOCC. It's a small bunch, maybe dozen people. Near as I can make out, they go around making trouble for anyone cutting cedar trees."

"Good luck with that," Oliver commented.

"All I know is you'd better have all the permits and be following every regulation in the book if they catch you cutting a stand of cedar. They've got a bunch of legal-beagles can tie you up in knots, otherwise."

"That would certainly get Ralph's goat, and Jack Fournier's, too," Oliver said. "What makes the cops suspect Ralph?"

"His chainsaw was left at the murder scene."

"You mean Carl was killed with a chainsaw, like in the movies?" Sarah said, picturing blood and gore flying everywhere.

"Not hardly," Pearly replied. "According to Charlie Howes, our very own sheriff, who got this from the Staties, somebody cut down a tree, and dropped it on Mueller. A big standing-dead beech. Mashed him flatter than a pancake."

"Wait a minute," Oliver said incredulously, "Are you telling me this Mueller guy stood around waiting while Ralph cut down a tree to squash him?"

"Hell no. The cops figure he was knocked out and dragged into position first."

"But why would Ralph leave his saw behind if he'd done it?" Sarah said.

"Someone who went to all the trouble of finding the right spot and getting his victim there wouldn't be likely to panic and forget his saw," Oliver added.

"Ralph is either an idiot, or he was framed." Sarah concluded.

"Why are you telling us all this?" Oliver asked.

Pearly gazed into his coffee mug. "I figured if we went up there and talked to Jack and his crew, the three of us could shake some sense into him about the tote road." He looked up and smiled benignly at them. "And you guys could maybe help poor Ralph out of his bind, being sort of amateur detectives, and all."

"Are you nuts?" Oliver demanded.

"We are *not* detectives, amateur or otherwise, and there's no way in the world we're going to meddle in a police investigation," Sarah exclaimed.

"You don't have to actually *do* anything," Pearly said. "Just reassure him that the cops will find the real killer. Tell him they've got nowhere near enough evidence to arrest him, and they're bound to be looking at other suspects. Poor Ralph is a basket case. He can't afford a lawyer or a private eye, and he doesn't know how the system works. Help him out and Jack may decide to be more reasonable about the tote road."

"What kind of twisted blackmail is that?" Oliver muttered.

"There must to be people who can help him with the legal stuff," Sarah said, "public defenders, legal aid."

"You want my advice?" Oliver said. "Go find some other cedar trees, and get somebody else to cut them."

"But those are nice big trees, hardly any knots, beautiful planking lumber. You can't hardly find cedar as good as those nowadays, and you're cutting for shares, so you'll get some of the boards."

Pearly looked at them hopefully. "Just come up and talk to them. Soothe their feathers, so Jack can cut the damn trees. Besides, I promised you'd come."

"Jesus, Gaites," Oliver growled.

"We leave now, we can be back by lunch," Pearly said, "and I'll have Eldon help you flip your boat."

"It's September. Shouldn't you be hauling boats out of the water?"

"It's low tide this morning," Pearly replied in a tone of voice which made it clear that he'd thought the situation through. "Can't haul boats out on a low tide."

_____

Chapter 4

Jack Fournier, "BB" Pearson, and Ralph Barnes, sat in a tight knot on one side of Ralph's round, formica-topped kitchen table, while Pearly, Oliver, and Sarah sat on the other.

Outside, a woman and two men stood across the road from Ralph's double-wide, waving placards and yelling whenever a car passed. The words, "Murderer! Tree killer!" filtered into the room.

"Jesus," Pearly said, "how long have those SOCC loonies been out there?"

"Ever since yesterday afternoon, when they found the body," Ralph replied. He looked haggard and depressed. "They stand around for three, four hours, then a car comes along, takes 'em away and leaves another bunch. I called the law on them, but all the cops did was chase them across the road."

"Pardon my French, but they're some pissed off about their head man being squashed like that," BB added.

"There was one of them TV news vans out there for a while first thing today," Jack added.

"SOCC probably tipped them off," Pearly muttered. "Good

publicity."

"We'd never do it," BB said, frowning out the window at the protesters, "but somebody's going to kill them people if they keep that up."

"I didn't kill anybody," Ralph said dispiritedly, as though he'd long since lost hope that anyone would believe his words.

Sarah looked at the three loggers. Jack, the head of the group, looked to be in his late fifties, with a week's worth of stubble on his chin and the weathered look of someone who had lived a hard life out of doors. BB Pearson, small and wiry, and looking to be in his forties, drove the skidder, while Ralph was tall, bald, and walked with a slight stoop as though weighed down by his seventy-two years.

Once again, Sarah wondered why she had let Pearly talk her into coming along. Had he wanted her here because her ex-husband was a lawyer? Was Pearly hoping she'd volunteer Claude's services? Pearly was on the wrong track in that case.

"What I don't see," Ralph said morosely, "is how them people found out 'bout me and the police in the first place."

They were less than two hours from the coast, but to Sarah's ears Ralph's short, clipped inland Maine accent was almost unintelligible after the coastal drawl.

"Ralph'd have to be dumber'n a stump to leave his saw behind anyhow," Jack said.

"How did they know it was your saw?" Oliver said.

"I scratched my name on it," Ralph replied. "Someone's trying to do me in, for sure."

"He couldn't have done it anyhow," BB said. "We was working almost two mile down the road from there. It would've taken old Ralph half a day to walk way up there into the puckerbrush on the back side of the Denton lot, drop a tree on that guy, and get back. And he was with us the whole time."

"Someone's trying to do me in," Ralph repeated.

It was beginning to look that way to Sarah, too.

"How did they find the body?" she said.

"Bangor paper said there was an anonymous tip," Jack replied. "Told them right where it was at. GPS numbers and everything."

A car passed outside, energizing the picketers, who waved their signs and chanted, "Murderer!" "Tree killer!" "Despoiler!"

Ralph slumped in his chair and sighed. "Don't know what I'm goin' to do. Irma couldn't stand having them people yelling and waving signs all day, so she's moved out to stay with our daughter and our two grandsons. For all I know they think I killed the damn fool."

"She don't think anything like that," Jack replied.

"I've half a mind to run 'em off for good," BB growled.

"Don't provoke them. That's what they want," Pearly said. "It will just make things worse."

"I don't understand the business with the saw," Oliver said. "How would somebody get a hold of it?"

"I figure somebody stole it out of my pickup while we was off in the woods," Ralph said. "I leave it right in the back."

"In the back?" Oliver said.

"She's got a cap on her," BB explained, "but there ain't no door, so anyone goin' by could have seen the saw."

"Wouldn't you have noticed if it was gone?" Sarah asked. "I mean, wouldn't you have needed it?"

"It was my backup saw," Ralph replied. "Don't take it out of the truck, 'less my good saw's broke."

"We didn't even know it was gone 'til the law came down on Ralph," Jack added.

A pickup truck went by to another chorus from outside. Ralph leaned on the table, his head in his hands. BB growled. Sarah seethed.

"We're going to do something about this," she said.

"We can't—" Oliver began, but Sarah ground her heel onto Oliver's toe under the table.

"Someone took the saw to snarl me up with the law is all I know," Ralph said, "but I don't see why, except those SOCC people gave us trouble a year back."

"Somebody might have decided that would make you a good candidate to frame for Carl's murder," Oliver said, "especially if they knew you were going to be cutting cedar around here."

Jack nodded. "Your cedar, up on the Denton lot, was right near where the SOCC guy got done in. I thought about that, but they wasn't making any trouble for us—"

"Yet," BB interjected.

"Somebody's sure making trouble for them, though, killin' that guy," BB concluded.

"Do the police know when he was killed?" Sarah said.

"They must figure 'round the middle of the morning," Ralph said. "At least that's when they wanted to know where I was at."

"I don't see how the police can pin it on you, then," Oliver said. "You've got an alibi. After all, you were with Jack and BB."

"Then why are they chasing after poor Ralph?" BB said.

"They're bound to question Ralph, because it's his saw, but that doesn't mean he's the only suspect," Oliver said reassuringly. "I'm sure they've got other suspects we don't know about."

"And you do have an iron-clad alibi," Sarah added.

Jack and BB seemed reassured by that, but Ralph, well endowed with typical Maine cynicism, looked unconvinced. "Maybe they figure we was all in on it," he said morosely.

"So what if they do?" Jack said. "They can't prove it."

"Besides," Sarah said, looking out the window, "there must be a lot of other people who have a grudge against SOCC. We'll put our heads together." She glanced at Oliver, daring him with her eyes to say anything.

Ralph nodded, looking more cheerful. "Guess that's the best I can hope for," he said. "I appreciate it."

There was a pause and Pearly said, "I've got to have that cedar, Jack."

"Oh, that," Jack said glibly. "The police had Bruce Nash cut a road in there yesterday, so they could get the body out. Goes right by them cedars you wanted."

"Skidder's just a mile down the road. We can get them trees out 'fore you know it," BB said.

Pearly struggled with his temper.

———

There was a chorus of chants as the three pseudo-sleuths started to get into Sarah's SUV. Sarah stopped and took out her cell.

"What are you doing?" Oliver said nervously.

"Let's just get out of here," Pearly urged.

"I'm going to take a picture of those creeps and put it in my album. It will fit right in with the shot I took of our back yard when the septic system blew up."

"Take Pearly's advice; don't make trouble," Oliver pleaded.

She smiled and blinked her eyes fetchingly. "Make trouble? Moi?"

Oliver groaned.

Sarah walked to the edge of the pavement and held up the cell. "Smile," she said to the picketers.

"Hey, what are you doing?" A short, balding aggressive-looking man in a new red-checkered L. L. Bean shirt demanded.

"Photographing some squirrels."

"Don't do this," Oliver said in an urgent stage whisper.

"You trying to harass us?" Checked-shirt said, starting across the road as he brandished his sign. "We got our rights."

"Are you threatening me with that sign?" Sarah replied. "Do I need to call 911?"

Checked-shirt stopped in his tracks and glared.

"What gives you the right to be judge and jury to a poor old man who didn't do anything?" Sarah went on. "What about *his* rights?"

Checked-shirt retreated to his companions, where they began their chanting and sign waving.

"Murderer! Tree killer! Forest despoiler!"

"Despoiler?" Sarah yelled at them. "How did you manage to cram that great big word into your teeny little brains?"

Her last broadside was muffled somewhat as Oliver and Pearly bundled her into the car.

"Why the hell did you take a picture of those idiots?" Pearly demanded as they pulled away from the now fist-shaking demonstrators.

"I don't know, except I thought it might aggravate them."

"Well, you succeeded," Oliver said.

"There ought to be a law against torturing a poor, innocent man like Ralph," Sarah grumbled.

"They're just exercising their right of free speech," Oliver pointed out.

"Well, they didn't like it much when I exercised mine," she replied, "but it made me feel better."

"It must be nice to be so sure of something that you know it has to be true no matter what the facts might say," Oliver mused.

"I'd like to shake some doubts into them," Pearly muttered.

"Not possible," Oliver replied. "They believe what they believe and facts don't enter into it. Especially facts that don't support what they want to think."

"I don't care what they believe," Sarah said. "We've got to help Ralph. Those people are ruining his life, driving his wife out of the house like that."

"I've met her," Pearly said, "and Irma isn't someone who drives easily. I can't see her wanting to stay with her daughter and those no-account grandsons, either." He shrugged. "Of course, the kid's father walked out when they were still toddlers, which probably had something to do with it."

"Why did Irma move out, then?" Oliver said. "Was it really about the picketers, or was she suspicious that Ralph killed Carl?" He turned to Sarah adding, "And what do you mean by offering to help Ralph? What was it you said about staying out of trouble that time I almost got my head shot off?"

"This is different."

"Sure it's different. This time we're dealing with homegrown fanatics, instead of imports."

"How can you look at what they've done to poor Ralph and turn your back?"

"We did cheer him up some," Pearly said.

"It would have saved us a trip if Jack had mentioned that the tote road problem was solved," Oliver grumbled.

"We know Ralph didn't do it," Sarah announced. "He doesn't strike me as the kind of person who would kill someone and leave his saw behind. Besides, what is his motive?"

"Could be most anything," Oliver said, playing the devil's advocate. "They admitted to having trouble with SOCC last year, and the three of them are a pretty close-knit bunch. Maybe they all got together to kill Mueller."

"And leave the chain saw behind?" Sarah retorted.

"Who else up there would have a grudge against SOCC?" Oliver countered.

"Maybe the landowner, if SOCC is slowing down the tree

cutting," Pearly said. "We could look into that."

Oliver frowned at Pearly.

"Jack and his crew are cutting nearby?" Sarah asked.

"About a mile or two from where Mueller was killed," Pearly replied.

"Do you suppose Bruce Nash would try to frame Jack's crew to stop them from cutting the cedar?" Sarah said.

"Can't see why," Pearly replied. "Nash has a big operation, lots of machinery to handle a big woodlot like that. A few cedars aren't going to mean much to him."

"It might be worth checking, even so," Sarah said.

"And how do you plan to do that?" Oliver said.

"How far is it to this Denton lot?" Sarah said.

"About ten minutes," Pearly replied.

"Might as well have a look while we're here," Sarah said.

Chapter 5

W hile Sarah was toying with SOCC's picketers outside of Ralph's house, her ex-husband was toying with his Porsche on Boston's Route 128. Claude cut across two lanes of traffic and took the Route 2 exit towards the city. His red 911 Turbo scrambled for traction as he wound down the exit ramp and accelerated south, the Porsche's exhaust making a satisfying howl as the engine spooled up.

Route 2 was two lanes each way, and traffic was light this time of day, so he expected to make good time.

Claude had a weakness for both fast cars and good-looking women, preferably women who's age was less than half his fifty-eight years. He was distinguished looking, with iron grey hair, and thanks to his gym membership, only a modest middle-aged spread. These physical attributes, along with an easy charm and deep pockets resulted in a lively dating life, made even livelier now that he was divorced and therefore free to see other women openly.

Lurlene Phipps happened to be both young and good looking, thereby meeting both of Claude's criteria, and he was talking to her on his no-hands cell as he cycled up through the gears.

One of the perks that came with being a successful attorney who was able to bring lucrative clients onto the firm's books was the freedom to take a warm pleasant Tuesday afternoon off, and Claude intended to do just that in the company of the shapely and seductive Lurlene.

Claude drove fast—that's why he'd bought the Porsche, after all—while he and Lurlene discussed plans for the afternoon and evening. They would, of course, end up in Claude's Back Bay apartment, but the choice of restaurant was proving to be difficult.

They tossed eating places back and forth like a pair of Little Leaguers warming up, and Claude was so absorbed by the conversation, and Lurlene's breathy voice, that he paid little attention to the box truck laboring up the hill ahead of him.

And the fact that its brake lights flashed at the hilltop.

Urged on by its 500 horsepower engine, The Porsche closed on the truck like a bullet—a very expensive bullet. Reveling in the car's nimbleness, Claude swung into the passing lane at the last second and shot by the truck just as they crested the hill.

The first thing he saw were bits of shredded tire in the roadway. The next thing he saw was a woman and two young children standing in the median, blocking any chance of escape.

The last thing he saw was the disabled SUV slewed across his lane.

———————

"Pull over here," Pearly said, indicating a level patch of ground beside an area of woods. "This is it, the old Denton home place."

"It's all trees and brush," Sarah said.

"This was field forty years ago," Pearly said. "The house was back in the woods a way."

"Why not put it next to the road?"

"This road probably wasn't here when the house was built," Pearly replied. "Besides, the old-timers usually built their houses where the land was good, not where the roads were."

"It's kind of sad," Sarah mused as she looked around.

"Times change," Pearly said simply. "Let's get out and see where Jack's new tote road is."

They found the road easily enough, a freshly rutted track, slicing into the woods and overlaid with crushed saplings and brush.

They followed the road, picking their way around the brush.

"Look over there," Oliver said after a while as he pointed up the road ahead of them.

Sarah could see a collection of heavy machinery parked in a clearing.

"Nash didn't waste any time getting his equipment in here," Pearly commented.

"What is it all?" Sarah asked, as she stared at the collection of oversized machines.

"The small ones," Oliver said, pointing to a pair of machines who's chain-encrusted tires were as tall as Sarah, "are called feller-bunchers. The jaws on the front grab a tree, and a big saw blade swings out of that box on the bottom to cut it down. The jaws also rotate so it can carry the tree away."

"The thing sounds kind of like a giant Skil saw when it's running," Pearly added. "They don't use chain saws all that much any more."

"The thing next in line is a wood chipper," Oliver went on. "Wood chips are in demand as biofuel."

Sarah recognized the chipper, an oversized version of the machines she often saw chopping up brush beside the roadways. The oversized device next to it was a mystery. "What does that thing do?" she inquired, looking curiously at the machine with its long crane-like arm.

"It's a timber harvester," Pearly replied. "That funny-looking thing on the end of the arm grabs a tree," Pearly explained, "and a saw on the bottom of it cuts the tree down, just like the smaller machines. But the harvester can turn the tree horizontal, and pull it tree through that top part, which cuts all the limbs off. At the same time it cuts the tree to whatever length you want and puts it on the pile."

"You have to see one in action to appreciate it," Oliver said.

"I'm not sure I want to."

"That thing can cut, limb, and stack a tree as quick as a bat in the night," Pearly added.

"And just how quick is that?"

"About a minute, or less."

"A tree a *minute?*" Sarah said in horror. "Maybe people like SOCC have a point. A tree a minute just doesn't seem right."

"It's a lot safer and quicker than cutting them down with a chain saw," Pearly commented.

Sarah frowned. "At least somebody is standing on the ground actually touching the tree when they use a chain saw. With these things they're just sitting on a cushy seat in a comfortable cab pushing levers. The poor tree doesn't have a chance."

Pearly gaped at her.

"I'm sorry, but it doesn't seem respectful of the tree," Sarah groused.

Just then, a man appeared from behind the harvester. He was wearing a John Deere cap and blue coveralls with the words, "Arden Forest Services" across the front.

"Here comes trouble," Pearly muttered.

"This land is posted," the man said cooly. "Didn't you see the signs? The police will arrest trespassers."

As the man drew nearer, Sarah could make out the name "Bruce" stitched below the left lapel.

"Well, Bruce," Pearly replied. "Jack Fournier is cutting a load of cedar for me in here."

"Good luck to you," Bruce said. "Him and his crew are tangled up with the law, so you'll probably have to wait a good while before you see your wood."

"Not all that long," Oliver commented.

"He'll be here tomorrow morning," Pearly added.

"Tomorrow?" Bruce said, obviously taken aback. "Are you sure?"

"Just spoke to him."

"Good," Bruce said, recovering from his surprise. "The sooner he gets his damn trees out of my way, the better. Can you believe the guy tried to get me to put in his access road for free?"

"Looks like you're getting some use out of it," Pearly commented.

"The cops paid me to put in that road," Bruce replied, glancing at his machinery, "and we'll start using it as soon as the police finish their investigating and the damn forester finishes fooling around with the trees."

Bruce turned to Pearly. "And you can tell Fournier that he'd better be here tomorrow because I don't want him puttering around with his damn cedars and getting in my way when we do start cutting."

Pearly eyed Arden Forest Services' machinery. "It must be costing you some to have that sitting around doing nothing."

Just then Sarah spotted a policeman appear from behind the timber harvester.

Bruce noticing her glance, said, "We hire off-duty cops to watch the machinery, discourage any vandalism."

"You have vandals way out here?" Sarah said.

"You never know what can happen out here," Bruce said, "like the head of SOCC being killed just up this tote road."

"Has SOCC been giving you trouble?" Oliver asked.

"We've had trouble with them in the past," Bruce said vaguely. "Most of those people come from the city or out of state, and they pretend to be experts on forestry. Half of them don't know a cedar tree from a fire hydrant, but they're able convince a lot of gullible flat-landers that there are no cedars left in Maine, and get them to donate to their cause."

Bruce looked at Sarah's expression and added, "I suppose they keep us honest, with all their picketing and lawsuits."

He turned to Pearly. "Your pal Fournier had better have all his paperwork in order, or SOCC will shut him down for sure."

"Jack isn't stupid," Pearly replied stiffly.

"He and his crew are a bunch of dubs," Bruce retorted. "They've been cutting corners with the law for years. For all I know, they haven't even filed the paperwork with the state to cut that cedar."

Bruce smiled at Pearly invitingly. "If you persuade old Derwin Denton to let us cut your trees, we can have them out a lot quicker than Fournier."

"Thanks, "Pearly said, "but I'm going to stay with Jack."

"You're taking a chance. The whole bunch of them could be in jail by tomorrow."

"What makes you think so?" Sarah said.

"It's obvious, isn't it? I'll bet Fournier's bunch got into a fight with SOCC over those cedars, ganged up on Carl Mueller, and killed him."

"That's one theory," Oliver said.

"It's the only one that makes sense."

———

"Friendly sort," Oliver commented when they were out of Bruce's hearing.

"He has a big problem," Pearly said.

"How so?" Sarah said.

"The timber harvester and all the rest of his equipment must add up to half-a-million dollars, second-hand," Pearly replied, "and Bruce can't make the bank payments on all that stuff unless it's working in the woods."

"A tree a minute," Sarah mused. "It must take a lot of land to keep them busy."

"That harvester can't handle really big trees, but it can sure cut a lot of wood," Pearly said. "Bruce may think small-time operators like Fournier are worthless, but all Jack has for heavy equipment is one beat-up John Deere skidder worth ten or fifteen grand on a good day. He can go in and do the small jobs that Bruce can't afford to touch."

———————

Dan Finlon was in his forties, with curly brown hair, which framed a round face, weathered by exposure to the outdoors. He'd worn a windbreaker and a blaze-yellow vest over his flannel shirt to ward off the cool morning air when he set out, and was getting ready to shed a layer when he came across Bruce Nash, standing next to the timber harvester.

"You all done mooning over the trees?" Bruce asked with heavy sarcasm. The pesky woman and her two friends had just left and Bruce was still fuming about the idea of having Jack Fournier underfoot tomorrow.

Dan gave Bruce an icy stare. "This isn't the only woodlot I'm managing," he replied. "I have a lot of other obligations besides taking care of you."

"Lighten up, for crying out loud," Bruce growled. "All I want to know is how much longer you're going to take before I can get to work in here. My crew could starve to death while I wait for you and the cops to finish tramping around in the woods."

"I'll be done when I'm done," Dan replied, deciding that he'd leave the windbreaker on for a while longer, at least until he was finished with Nash.

"What the hell is taking you so long? They're just trees, dammit. Didn't Denton tell you to speed it up?"

Dan had a small backpack, which contained his miscellaneous tools, water bottle, and snack food. He shrugged the pack into a more comfortable position. "A few more days," he said.

"Jesus. A few more days? Couldn't you at least let us start cutting the places you've gone over?"

"Have you ever had SOCC on your case? All they need is one cedar tree and they're on you like a swarm of black flies. I'm not taking any chances with those fanatics looking for any excuse to make trouble."

Bruce swore under his breath. "You let me worry about them."

Dan looked at Bruce speculatively. He felt cooler now that he was standing still. "One of them has been killed already," he said. "You don't want to make threats at this point."

Bruce gave Dan an angry look.

"Look," Dan said, trying to sound reasonable, "I work for the landowner, Derwin Denton—"

"You mean his grandson, don't you?"

"—and I have to protect his best interests. And that means making sure that people like SOCC can't find an excuse to tie us up in court. Do you want the sheriff to come out here and shut you down because SOCC has found some hokey violation?"

"Speaking of violations, you had some bad luck with SOCC last year, didn't you?" Bruce said nastily. "That was Jack Fournier and his crew, wasn't it? Made some mistakes laying out the tote roads? Came too close to a brook, didn't you?"

"I seem to remember that you got carried away a while back and cut too many trees on a woodlot over in Monroe. Didn't SOCC get you for an illegal clear-cut?" Dan retorted.

They glared at each other for a moment before Bruce shrugged, saying, "Look, we both want the same thing: to get this woodlot cut off. And from what I hear, you need the money as much as I do, maybe more."

Dan, still frowning, nodded agreement.

"SOCC is the problem here," Bruce went on, his voice reasonable. "For both of us. Okay, so they've dinged both our reputations over the years."

Dan nodded again, staring off into the woods.

"The way I see it," Bruce said, "we're both in the same boat, so we might as well work around SOCC any way we can."

Dan looked at his companion grimly. "All those bastards live for is to make trouble; they don't really give a damn about protecting cedar trees."

"It's all about power to them," Bruce agreed. "We have a right to make a living. Those guys will run us out of the woods for good if we don't stand up to them, even if we have to get rough."

Dan took a step backwards, holding up his hands. "I don't want to get into anything illegal—"

"I'm not asking you to." Bruce leaned forward earnestly. "Just let us start cutting in someplace you've already gone over. Give my men a chance to feed their families."

Bruce paused, his face grim. "I'll take the heat if SOCC comes around. I'll give them enough trouble so they won't bother you at all."

Dan smiled at his new ally for the first time. "I've flagged a route for an access road from here over to the far side of the lot, away from where the cops are, about a half-mile in from the paved road. There's about 150 acres, a nice stand of pine, some birch, and some pulp wood. Should keep you busy for a while. We can walk over it this afternoon, and I'll tell you what I have in mind."

"However you want to do it is fine with me," Bruce said, clapping Dan on the shoulder. "Thanks, and believe me, you won't regret this."

"Just one thing," Dan replied. "Don't let your road wander away from my flagging, or you'll get too close too the boggy spot in there."

"I know the regulations," Bruce huffed.

"I'm just saying," Dan held up his hands placatingly. "And for god's sake, don't go cutting outside that area until I've finished or the tree-huggers will find an excuse to give us hell."

"No problem. Today is what, Tuesday? Fournier is supposed to be getting that damn cedar out tomorrow, so we'll move in first thing Wednesday. Maybe with the cedar gone, SOCC will leave us alone."

"Don't you wish," Dan replied.

Chapter 6 _____

"Why on earth do you want to find the old Denton house?" Pearly said incredulously as they made their way down the tote road. "The place must have burned down thirty years ago. There's nothing left but an old cellar hole."

"I'd still like to see it," Sarah said stubbornly.

Oliver gave her a worried look. "Why? It can't have anything to do with Carl's murder."

"I just want to take a look before we leave."

"Be a hell of a thing to find in all this brush," Pearly muttered, "and I'm not sure exactly where it was anyway."

They spent the better part of twenty minutes pushing their way through a jungle of saplings and underbrush, with Pearly grumbling to himself, before they spotted a dead apple tree.

"Must be getting close," Pearly said. "There was an old orchard in back of the house."

Soon, they came upon a huge, shrub-choked lilac.

"It's got to be right around here," Pearly said. "The old-timers loved to have a lilac in the back yard."

They pushed through more brush, and nearly fell into the cellar hole.

Shrubs and sapling overhung the void and the stone forming part of one wall had fallen in. Sarah looked at the dead leaves and bits of trash lining the bottom—an oversized grave, full of lost lives and memories. Suddenly, her mind flashed back to the spring when she had stood over the cellar hole of Myra Huggard's newly burned out house—the smell of charred wood and decay, the knowledge that Myra had died there.

Sarah lurched back, shocked by the vividness of her memory. Was this some kind of PTSD? Perhaps Claude had been right to fuss about the murders she'd been caught up in this summer.

Oliver looked at her, worry in his eyes. "Maybe we should go back to the car."

Sarah wondered if he'd sensed the intensity of her reaction. "The cellar is so little," she said in a small voice. She could hear the reassuring sound of a car passing by on the road a few hundred yards away.

"Houses were small in those days," Pearly pointed out.

A picture formed in her mind of the Dentons, huddled around the fireplace on a cold winter's night, an icy wind whistling through the foundation stones. "It's sad," she said, "thinking about generations of Dentons dedicating their lives to this piece of land, and now this is all that's left."

"What do you mean, sad?" Pearly retorted. "It was a hell of a life, trying to farm this land. This isn't like up in the County, where there's good soil to work. They were probably starving and got out of here because they found something better. You sound like old Derwin, clinging to the past."

"Do you know him?" she asked.

"I know people like him. I know how they think. I know old Derwin is an idealist who wouldn't let that woodlot be cut for the past forty years, and probably wouldn't have the land cut off now if he had a choice."

"Why doesn't he have a choice?"

"Because he's in a nursing home, and it's costing him an arm and a leg."

"Where's the nursing home?"

"Don't tell her," Oliver warned.

"Yarmouth, if I remember right," Pearly said.

"Maybe we should go and call on him," Sarah said.

"Maybe we shouldn't," Oliver replied.

"I could go down and do some shopping at the outlets," she mused, ignoring Oliver, and unaware that her plans were about to be disrupted.

———

It was late afternoon by the time Pearly had left Sarah and Oliver in Oliver's shop and headed home. Sarah stood back and admired *Daisy's* bottom. She was glad the boat had a name now, even though it was still just an unfinished hull, lying upside down on a series of supporting legs like a huge centipede.

The freshly fiberglassed hull glistened in the afternoon sun, and Sarah couldn't help feeling a sense of pride in her handiwork.

"What comes next?" she asked.

"We'll long-board it to sand out the bumps and hollows," he said, presenting her with a flexible, four-foot board, covered with sandpaper.

"This is a long-board?"

"Right. It's flexible enough to follow the shape of the hull, and long enough to bridge the hollows."

It didn't take long for Sarah to discover that long-boarding was hard work, as the two of them toiled away with their boards.

"About this morning, at that cellar hole. . ." Sarah began. "It was so vivid. . ."

"You looked shook. Could it have just been a delayed reaction to seeing Myra's cellar hole this spring?"

"It's got to be more than that. It's got to be resonating with something. I just don't know what."

"You need a vacation," he said.

"This summer was supposed to be my vacation," she said brusquely. "Claude doesn't approve of you, you know. Not that his opinion matters. He keeps reminding me that I never got involved with killers before I met you. He calls you a murder magnet."

"*Me* a murder magnet? Did you tell him that *I* never got involved with killers until you came along?"

They worked in silence for a while.

"How about renting a place somewhere around here if you can't stay in the Merlews granny flat?" Oliver said.

"I'm not sure I want to do that."

"You could use the guest room here. I can be very proper and chaste."

"Oh, like that would last for long," she said with a snort.

"I have great self control."

"Maybe *you* do."

Oliver stopped sanding and looked at her solemnly. "Do you want to stay in Maine at all, then?"

"I don't know what I want to do," she moaned. "I came to Maine this spring to have some peace and quit, so I could figure out what I wanted to do after the divorce." She glared at Oliver. "But thanks to you and all that's been happening, there hasn't been time to think about anything."

"Things always slow down around here in the fall."

"You're a distraction all by yourself. I just haven't had time—"

She was interrupted by her cell's chime.

"Where are you?" Jeff demanded, a note of desperation in his voice. Her son sounded so much like her ex that it always startled Sarah.

"I'm in Maine, of course."

"You mean nobody called?" Sarah could hear the tension in his voice.

"Called about what?"

"Dad had an accident this morning."

Dread flooded over Sarah. "In his car?"

"Where else? He drives like a lunatic." Jeff made an exasperated noise. "Lurlene said she would call you, but I suppose that was expecting too much."

"Lurlene has never, ever spoken to me, Jeff."

"She was okay this morning when she called, but she's having hysterics now," he said dryly. "They put her on medication an hour ago."

So, Lurlene, a.k.a. "Lolita the child slut" was having hysterics? Sarah suppressed a feeling of smug satisfaction. "Was she hurt in the accident, too?"

"God, no. she wasn't in the car, but she was talking to Dad on the phone when it happened."

"Oh," Sarah said, pulling herself together. "How bad is it?"

"A broken left leg, compound fracture of the right arm, and head injuries," Jeff paused, his voice shaky. "The car glanced off an SUV, flipped end over end, landed on its roof." He paused again. "They did emergency surgery to relieve the pressure on his brain, but he still hasn't regained consciousness, so they don't know—"

Sarah didn't feel as though she was doing a very good job of getting up to speed on the situation. "Where are you," she asked.

"Mass General. Lurlene called me around the middle of the day, and I managed to get a flight out of JFK right away. I just arrived here." Jeff paused again and Sarah could hear the familiar background noises of a busy hospital.

"I talked to sis," he went on, "but I don't think she'll come, so long as Lurlene is in the picture. You know she hasn't spoken to Dad since the divorce."

"What about Lurlene's family?"

"No help there. Her family are all on the west coast, and it doesn't sound as though they're likely to come here to Boston to hold their daughter's hand."

There was another, longer pause. "I've got to get back to New York in a day or two, to my job," Jeff said. "There's nobody else to help around here, and God knows how Dad is going to come out of this."

Sarah swore under her breath, looked at her watch. "I'll meet you there around nine this evening."

She broke the connection and turned to meet Oliver's worried eyes. "Trouble?" he said.

"Claude has had a car accident." Her voice sounded unsteady in her ears. "There may be brain damage."

He took her in his arms for a while as she sobbed out her fear, frustration, and anger.

At last she stepped away. "I have to go down, at least until he's out of the woods." *If he comes out of the woods.*

"Of course."

"Jeff has to get back to his job in New York, and there's nobody else to look after him."

"Yes," Oliver said softly, and paused before adding, "What about his girlfriend? Was she hurt too?"

"She wasn't in the car."

"Can she help?"

"Lurlene is a waste of perfectly good oxygen," Sarah replied.

Oliver looked at her, confused. "Then what does he see in her?"

"Eye candy."

"Yes, but surely—"

Sarah interrupted him with a kiss. "I could get to like you a lot, even if you are a murder magnet," she said after a moment.

"Likewise." He paused, adding, "And there's always the spare room."

Chapter 7

Claude's face looked as though he'd gone ten rounds with Mohammad Ali. The rest of his head was wrapped in bandages, while his left leg and his right arm were in casts. With all the coverings, he looked like something from an Egyptian tomb, only not as well preserved.

"The face is superficial, from the air bag," Jeff murmured. "He hasn't regained consciousness yet, but he moved his good arm a little, about an hour ago. I guess that's a good sign."

Sarah had first met her ex-husband in a hospital, where she had been a nurse and he was recovering from surgery for a ruptured appendix. Of course, he'd been some thirty-five years younger then, witty, full of life and fun.

Foolishly, she'd half expected him to be full of life now, at least partly. Certainly not the bruised, inert form in this bed.

She swayed unsteadily, and Jeff caught her arm. "Maybe we should go down to the cafeteria and get some coffee."

"Yes," she said, dully, thinking that her day had begun at dawn in Oliver's bed some fifteen yours ago, and sleep was still a very long way off. "It's been a long day."

The vending machine coffee lived up to her worst expectations, but at least it was hot and strong. The cafeteria was almost deserted at this time of the night, except for a white-coated group seated at one of the circular plastic tables, and a lone woman slumped in a corner.

"Damn," Jeff said, "that's Lurlene. I thought they had put her in a bed somewhere."

The woman looked up and waved. "Jeffie, over here," she said, her voice slurred.

Jeff paused for a moment, looking like an amateur chemist nervously contemplating the mixture two explosive compounds.

Sarah sighed, took a deep swallow from her paper cup, placed it on a convenient table, and advanced on Lurlene.

"Mom!" the girl exclaimed happily, a grin splitting her face.

Sarah studied at her ex's girlfriend, who looked about sixteen, but was really in her twenties. She was wearing a tight cashmere sweater and a mini-skirt designed to display as much leg as was legally permissible. If there was any justice in the world, Sarah though grimly, the child would get frostbite when she want outside and end up having her legs amputated.

Lurlene wobbled to her feet and half embraced, half fell on Sarah. Her breath was a fire hazard. Whatever the cup on the table contained, it was a lot stronger than coffee.

"Mom," Lurlene sobbed.

"I am not your mother," Sarah informed her.

After a period of clinging and sobbing, Lurlene mumbled, "Now that you're here, I think I'll go home." Her diction was fading fast.

"Like hell you will," Sarah retorted, as she unhooked one of the girl's arms and removed the shoulder bag.

"Get her car keys," Sarah told Jeff, handing him the purse.

He rooted around Lurlene's handbag, muttering, "I'm not too good with ladies purses."

"For god's sake, how hard can it be to find a set of keys?"

"Oh, look," Lurlene chirped at Jeff, her eyes wide, "Your purse looks just like mine."

Lurlene had both arms wrapped around Sarah's neck again and was hanging on her like a drunken baboon. "She won't last much longer with all that booze on top of whatever sedative they gave her," Sarah told Jeff. "You'd better find a nurse."

Jeff emerged triumphantly with a set of keys and handed them to Sarah.

"Do you have a car, too?" Lurlene asked Sarah in a voice filled with wonder.

"I have a helicopter gunship," Sarah snapped.

"Oooh, how nice," Lurlene said, with an owlish stare. "I wonder if Clausy Baby would get me one."

"Of course he would," Sarah assured her, observing Lurlene's dilated pupils. Surely the girl would pass out soon. "They're such fun," Sarah added sweetly, "and a pink one would go well with your outfit."

Jeff stared at his mother nervously.

"Get someone *now*," she growled at him. "And make sure the nurse brings a wheelchair."

"Yes," Lurlene said dreamily, "flying through the air—" With that, she collapsed against Sarah.

"Correction: a Gurney," Sarah said.

———

Sarah called her daughter from Claude's room, but Jean was adamant.

"I am *not* flying in from Chicago," she said, "so long as Loose Hips Phipps is anywhere around. I won't go within a hundred yards of that little home-wrecker. I'd probably strangle her if I did."

Lurlene a home-wrecker? Sarah wished it was that simple, but it wasn't, and she didn't feel up to trying to explain it all to Jean. Again.

"Look," Sarah said, "All I'm saying is—"

Claude groaned, and opened his eyes.

"I'll call you back," Sarah said. "Dad looks like he's waking up."

Jeff pushed the call button, saying, "We're supposed to get a doctor as soon as he comes around."

Sarah leaned over the bed, checked his eyes. "Claude, do you know who I am?"

He reached up with his good arm and caressed her cheek. "You are my lovely wife."

"Ex-wife, you dolt."

Claude seemed to grope for a word. "Technicalities," he said finally. "Thanks for being here."

"Do you know what happened?"

"Wrecked my car."

"He's fine," she said to Jeff.

Claude's hand dropped to her breast. "I love you," he murmured.

Sarah removed his hand. "Get your paw off me, you lecherous, two-timing Lothario before I slap what's left of your brain into mush," she said.

The smile of relief on her face belied the words. That and the fact she was still holding his hand.

Sarah knew all too well that medical tests could still uncover some subtle brain damage, and a long recovery could lie ahead, but the essential Claude appeared to still be there. For better or for worse.

A nurse entered and chased Sarah and Jeff out of the room,

saying, "Why don't you two get some coffee while the doctor checks out our patient."

"Irish coffee for me," Claude replied drowsily.

Chapter 8 _____

The town of Tyler was only thirty miles from the coast, but it was light-years away in most other respects. Dee's ramshackle country store occupied the town's only intersection, in stark contrast to the bustling coastal towns' upscale shops. Instead of well-heeled tourists, Tyler's residents were primarily trees.

The early morning air had a bite to it, hinting that frost would be coming soon. The hard-packed dirt parking lot beside Dee's Country Store was filled with an assortment of cars and pickups, several of recent vintage and expensive pedigree. The lot overlooked a low, swampy area where scattered maples were showing color.

Ken Pourier was in his late forties and was rapidly losing his straight, dark hair, to his dismay. He stood at one side of the small crowd and took in the scene. About fifteen people stood around the lot, most holding cups of coffee from the store. He reflected with a heady thrill that with Carl dead, he was now the leader of SOCC and these were his people. Ken intended to make changes in the organization, and picketing Ralph Barnes was just a start.

Sal Demano sidled up. He was in his early thirties, with dark, longish hair, a long face, and dark jumpy eyes.

"A good turnout," Sal commented. "We got a couple of newcomers over there," he added nodding across the lot. "I talked to them and they seem interested in being active members of the group, if you get my drift."

"I do, and I think that's just the kind of thing we need to start doing more of. Carl's death may be a blessing in disguise if it energizes the Cause."

Sal glanced at his watch. "Almost time to fire them up," he said giving Ken a friendly punch on the arm. "Just let me know what you need."

Ken watched Sal wander off to work the crowd. He didn't know much about the young man except that he came from Boston's North End, had joined SOCC in the spring, and had hinted that his uncle was "connected." He also knew that Sal was in the import business of some kind, that he traveled around the state, and was a genius at finding supporters with money.

Most important of all, Sal shared Ken's vision of turning SOCC into a statewide presence through picketing, demonstration, and the kind of activism that skirted the law when that became necessary to achieve their goals.

Carl's reluctance to push the boundaries of activism had been a sore point with Ken, and he saw Carl's death as a golden opportunity to set a new course.

Ken, acutely conscious that he wasn't a particularly tall or imposing man, climbed onto the bed of his pickup and banged on the cab's roof to attract everybody's attention.

"I want to thank you all for turning out on this nippy morning," Ken began, trying to drown out a few stubborn talkers in the crowd. "I know you're all upset about Carl's murder, but I assure you that his death will not be in vain. It will not be in vain!"

Ken waited for the shouting to die down. "I know you're angry at the thoughtless, greedy people who put money ahead of our forests. Ahead of *our heritage!*'

Ken knew he was preaching to the choir, and he felt an almost erotic sense of power as he worked the people into a frenzy of shouting.

After a few more minutes of exhortation, Ken dropped his voice. He had their rapt attention now. "A stand of cedar trees were cut down yesterday afternoon," he said in a tone of grief and righteous indignation.

Shouts of anger echoed across the parking lot, and Ken noted with satisfaction that several store patrons were listening with interest. He raised his hands to silence the mob.

"And we are going to mourn those trees! And we're going to show the world just how unhappy we are with the greedy fat-cats who are raping *our* forests! And murdering those who stand in their way!"

The rage was almost palpable now, and Ken had a twinge of fear that he had gone too far. He looked around, noticed Sal standing nearby, giving him a thumbs-up. Again, Ken raised his hands for silence.

"We are going to honor Carl's memory by staging a *peaceful* demonstration—" A chorus of boos and catcalls greeted the emphasis on peaceful.

"A *PEACEFUL* demonstration, as befits the memory of a noble man and a noble tree!"

The Reverend Leonard Briskin lived a double life. When he wasn't tending his flock at the Arms of Salvation Full Gospel church, the beefy, middle-aged cleric drove an eighteen-wheel pulp truck as a way to supplement his income.

Pastor Briskin found an elegant symmetry in this lifestyle. By leading God's bounty, namely trees, to their higher calling, namely the mill, he was serving God's will—and incidentally feeding his family. That, in turn, enabled him to lead his flock to their higher calling, namely salvation.

And so it was with a feeling of satisfaction and mission that Pastor Briskin deftly maneuvered his truck up the newly-made tote road to a pile of cedar trees.

He observed that it was a modest pile, less than half a load.

He also observed that a group of men and women, wearing black arm-bands, were standing beside the trees. One of them, a shortish dark-haired man, was holding a bible and apparently leading the group in prayer—a situation that aroused Pastor Briskin's professional interest.

Not wanting to intrude on a religious service, however heathenish it appeared to be, he silently dismounted and clambered up a metal ladder, which led to the top of a pedestal behind the cab. Here was located a small seat and a set of controls for the big hydraulic log-loading arm.

The arm's movement as it lifted slowly from the truck's bed, energized the crowd.

"Despoiler! Raper of the forest! Tree killer!" they screamed.

The crowd's choice of words did not sit well with Pastor Briskin.

They fell silent as Briskin stood and glared down at them from his perch some fifteen feet overhead.

It was an imposing sight, for the man was well over six feet tall, and tipped the scales at nearly two-hundred pounds. With his tousled hair, blowing in the cool morning breeze, his rampantly bushy eyebrows, which bristled ominously with indignation, his three-day beard, scruffy sweatshirt and jeans, Pastor Briskin looked like a modern-day John the Baptist. One could almost imagine that the Hannaford Supermarket shopping bag—which reposed in the truck's cab and held his lunch—contained a helping of locusts and honey, in addition to a can of diet Coke.

"I shall pray for you miserable sinners!" he bellowed in a voice that seemed to shake the very ground. "You, who would worship a handful of trees instead of your Creator will be dammed to eternal hellfire!"

A few more paragraphs along those lines and Pastor Briskin started to get warmed up. He pointed a prophetic finger at the bible in Ken Pourier's hand. "You, holding that bible!" he thundered. "Have you ever opened the Good Book?! Have you ever read where it says in Genesis that God made creation for the use of Human-kind?!"

The people around Ken sidled away, leaving their leader to squirm under the heat of Briskin's gaze.

"Those trees are a precious gift from God, given for our use! And yet you pray over them as though they were idols! Would you turn your back on God's gifts?!"

A few of the protestors muttered, shifting uncomfortably.

Further up the tote road, the off-duty cop stationed by Arden Forest Services' motor pool, could hear Pastor Briskin's booming voice. He began to worry, and thought for a moment of calling in for backup, but decided to wait a little longer in hopes it would blow over.

"Does that Bible feel hot in your hand?!" The fiery cleric demanded.

Ken fingered his Bible nervously, as though it did suddenly feel uncomfortably warm.

"That's the heat of God's righteous anger! Repent! Repent! Repent, or you will surely burn for eternity!"

Looming over his audience, Pastor Briskin lowered his voice to a mere shout.

"In your sin and ignorance, you may pray for these trees, like heathen idolaters, but *I* will pray for your Immortal Souls!"

Sal Demano took this opportunity to begin SOCC's official chant. "Tree killer! Forest despoiler!" he shouted from the back of the crowd. Gradually, the others took up his refrain.

Having said his piece, Pastor Briskin sat and brought the arm's jaws over the first log.

Two protestor promptly climbed onto the log, chanting their well-worn words.

"I will pray for your bodies and souls as I go about God's work!" Pastor Briskin informed them.

Clamping the arm's jaws around one end of the log, he skillfully gave it a shake, dislodging the protestors, who tumbled to the ground like ants shaken off a picnic potato chip.

The off-duty cop, hearing that screams of rage were replacing shouts of exhortation, began hiking, somewhat reluctantly, towards the noise.

The tree-loading process became a choreographed event: the Jaws of Justice would descend on a log, a group of protestors would climb on it, Pastor Briskin would shake them off, load the log, and the strange dance would repeat itself, accompanied by shouts and oaths.

All parties must come to an end, however, and with the off-duty cop discouraging further violence, and the logs safely on his truck, Pastor Briskin clambered into the cab. A few hardy souls stood to block the truck's way, but wisely moved back on hearing the words, "I will pray for your bodies and souls as I do God's work!"

———

Ken was deeply disappointed that his carefully arranged protest hadn't gone as planned. He should never have let that bible-thumping trucker get the upper hand. Who could have predicted a disaster like that?

He was even more disappointed that the Channel 5 TV News van hadn't arrived until after the pulp truck was gone, thereby depriving SOCC of a golden photo-op. What had taken them so damn long to get here?

While the protestors gathered around the belated TV van, eager to tell their tale of mistreatment, one member of SOCC was missing, for Sal Demano's black Chevy Impala had followed Pastor Briskin's truck towards its destination.

Chapter 9

While Pastor Briskin was exhorting SOCC from his pulp-truck pulpit, Sarah was some two hundred miles to the south, sitting in the bay-windowed breakfast nook of her house in Sudbury, Massachusetts, while she shared coffee with her friend and next-door neighbor Muffy Willet.

"Did you get any sleep at all last night?" Muffy said worriedly as she studied Sarah's face across the round butcher-block table.

"About four hours."

Sarah and Jeff had driven out of Boston in the wee-small hours to Sudbury, stopping to pick up a few groceries on the way.

The house had been dark when they arrived. They turned on the lights, found the rooms looking forlorn and smelling musty, the air thick with years of memories—memories that had begun with joy and promise, and ended with disillusionment and divorce.

"You look awful," Muffy commented, jolting Sarah out of her gloomy thoughts.

Good old Muffy, never afraid to say what she thought, even to the point of displaying her unconscious prejudices. Sarah figured the "awful" comment wasn't just her crow's feet, but included her sweatshirt and worn jeans in contrast to Muffy's perfectly tailored linen jacket and designer slacks. But then Sarah hadn't been able to summon the energy to dress up to Sudbury standards this morning. And wasn't sure she cared. "It's nothing a good night's sleep won't fix," Sarah replied.

"Where's Jeff?" Muffy asked.

"I dropped him off at the T this morning so he could visit Claude for a few hours. I'll drive in around noon to visit Claude and take Jeff into Logan so he can catch his flight back to New York this afternoon."

Muffy looked at Sarah questioningly.

"I just wanted to putter around the house this morning, tidy things up and air out the rooms."

Muffy nodded. That, she could understand. Musty rooms were not to be tolerated in Muffy's world. Still. . .

"How is he?" Muffy said.

"They ran a bunch of tests last night, and there doesn't seem to be any serious brain damage, just short term amnesia around the accident. It may be a while before we know for sure."

"And he has a broken leg?"

"Plus a broken arm."

"It's going to be a long haul to get him back on his feet," Muffy commented.

"Tell me about it," Sarah said. It was a thought that had been preying on her mind ever since she'd gotten Jeff's phone call.

"What about Lurlene? Can she help?"

"The girl was so smashed on tranquilizers and booze last night that they had to wheel her out of the cafeteria on a Gurney."

"The poor child," Muffy said, "it must have been a shock."

"I suppose it was," Sarah agreed reluctantly.

"Maybe with a little work, she can be whipped into shape."

"I didn't bring a whip."

Muffy nodded with a sigh. "There's really not much to her, beyond looks. It's too bad, because somebody will have to take care of him."

"Why are you looking at me?" Sarah demanded.

"He was your husband and the father of your children," Muffy said mildly.

Sarah almost envied Muffy. Life was so simple for her. Everything boiled down to matters of duty, of clearly defined questions of right and wrong. Gray just didn't seem to be in the woman's color scheme.

"It would make sense for him to recuperate out here where it's quiet, and the house has plenty of room," Muffy went on relentlessly, "and you used to be a nurse."

"That was thirty-five years ago, and I am *not* turning my house into a rehab center for Claude and his dizzy bimbo," Sarah retorted.

Seeing she had hit a brick wall, Muffy changed course. "I wish you didn't look so tired. What have you been doing all summer?"

How to answer Muffy's innocent question? In fact, Sarah had spent the summer on a steady diet of murder and mayhem, all of which, she feared, was cascading towards an impending meltdown. The vividness of her flashback at the cellar hole had scared her—and still scared her. And that wasn't counting her involvement with Oliver. For Muffy's sake, Sarah chose a policy of deceit. "The summer has been a change of pace, but very busy," she replied, "and I am tired."

"I hope you're going to stay here for a while and get some rest," Muffy said sympathetically. She was quiet for a moment before adding, "Did you know there's been a car parked at the end of your driveway all morning?"

"I can't see the end of my driveway from here."

"Well I can from my living room window, and it made me nervous. That's why I brought the car instead of walking. I gave him the eye when I drove in and he took off. But I did get his licence plate number." Muffy held up her cell phone triumphantly, showing the rear end of a car, its plate clearly visible.

Sarah wrote down the number.

"You should call the police," Muffy advised. "I hate to see cars parked like that in this neighborhood, especially with all the burglaries going on."

———————

Oliver's house, a weathered, 1850's vintage colonial, sat on the flank of Hound Hill where it overlooked a scrubby hayfield. At right angles to the house was a large barn, which had been converted to a boatbuilding shop. It was mid-afternoon by the time Pearly's logs arrived at Oliver's place and the truck had maneuvered its way behind the barn-cum-boatshop to the sawmill.

With the logs piled on the brow of the mill, Pastor Briskin paused and looked worriedly at Oliver. "People leak, brother Oliver," he rumbled. "Salvation seeps out of them like sweat on a summer day."

"I suppose it does, but—"

"People leak," the cleric repeated, building up a head of steam, "and that's why we must come to Jesus to be refilled with God's Grace."

"I'm sure we do, but—"

Pastor Briskin leaned forward and gazed into Oliver's eyes. "And that is why I have prayed for God to lead you to our humble church." He shook his head sadly. "We haven't seen you since you found salvation that day on Pemaquid Point."

"It wasn't exactly—"

"We must listen to the Lord, and go where he leads us, and I hear Him calling to you, brother Oliver."

"I've had busy summer."

"I'm not concerned about the worries of a single summer, my brother; I'm concerned about choosing between an eternity of salvation, or an eternity in the nether regions."

Oliver felt a sense of relief when their conversation was interrupted as two cars pulled up behind the pulp truck.

Pastor Briskin stared balefully the group emerging from their vehicles. "The Lord has chosen to visit a plague of locusts upon us, brother Oliver."

Wes, who was sleeping by Oliver's feet, leaped up to greet the newcomers, barking and cavorting circles around them. Several shrank back nervously.

"SOCC," Oliver replied.

"You know them."

"We met them picketing at Ralph Barnes' house. The leader's name is Ken something-or-other, according to the newspaper."

"I prayed for that heathen horde as I drove over here, and Jesus reminded me that I must love them despite their strange ways."

The group, about half a dozen, advanced, and Ken said to Oliver, "I recognize you. You were at Ralph Barnes' place yesterday. The woman with you took our picture." Ken turned to Pastor Briskin. "And you're the goddam truck driver who made all that trouble for us this morning. Well you're going to pay for that. You think you're pretty smart, but you're just another stooge for the fat-cat timber barons."

"Timber barons?" Oliver murmured in bemusement.

Pastor Briskin inhaled, and abruptly turned his back on the SOCC'ers. "Brother Oliver," he murmured, ignoring Ken's angry glare, "we must be gentle with these poor, ignorant souls." Turning to face Ken he said, "What brings you here, my brothers and sisters?"

"We've come hold a funeral for the trees you helped destroy,"

Ken replied pugnaciously. "The funeral you interrupted earlier today."

Pastor Briskin's eyebrows lifted shaggily at this. "A funeral? Have you found an appropriate passage from Scripture to read over these noble logs, these gifts from God, brother Ken? A passage that reflects their rightful place in the Good Book?"

"What?"

"Perhaps a reading from the 104th Psalm: 'The trees of the LORD are full of sap; the cedars of Lebanon, which He hath planted.'" Pastor Briskin paused, reflecting. "Or maybe a passage from First Kings: 'So he built the house, and finished it; and covered the house with beams and boards of cedar.'"

"We're here to mourn *these* trees," Ken retorted, "not listen to a bunch of bible thumping about Lebanon."

Pastor Briskin collected himself with an effort. "I have prayed for you this morning, my brothers and sisters, that you may learn to celebrate these gifts, as they go on to better things, to their higher purpose. Just as God gave us Gopher wood to build the Ark and the great cedars of Lebanon to build the temple—"

"Gopher wood?" one of the SOCC'ers said.

Pastor Briskin paused in preparation for a dissertation on Gopher wood, but Sal, in the back of the group, slipped once again into his role as cheerleader.

"Tree killer! Forest despoiler!"

Pastor Briskin sighed heavily. "The True Believer always seems to prefer ignorance to enlightenment," he muttered to Oliver. "We must pray for them, even so. We must never give up hope."

"*They* certainly don't give up."

"They have a strange way of showing grief," Pastor Briskin commented over the din.

"I'm going to call 911 and get them out of here."

"I can save you the trouble," Briskin said, glancing the cars parked in front of his truck. "These people know me," he added.

Clambering onto the truck's running board, he addressed the crowd. "I will pray for your bodies and souls as I go about my work today!"

The group fell silent and looked with growing alarm at the truck as it began to inch its way towards their cars.

"I'll call a wrecker," Oliver assured them.

A long blast from the truck's air horn sent the SOCC'ers scrambling for their cars.

"How is he doing?" Sarah asked Jeff as she looked down at Claude's sleeping form. The swelling on his face seemed to be down, though it looked even more black-and-blue than yesterday.

"I think he's better," Jeff said uncertainly. "He wakes up and is pretty with it—a little confused about some things, but not too bad. Then, after a while, he gets grouchy and monosyllabic, and goes to sleep again. I suppose it's his head."

"Has the doctor been in to see him this morning?"

"He seemed to think Dad was doing okay." Jeff paused. "Dad's been telling me about this boyfriend you have. A boatbuilder?"

"He designs them, too. You're spending too much time listening to Claude, when he doesn't know all the facts. Don't forget, my father was a carpenter. I wasn't born with a silver spoon in my mouth, like Claude."

Seeing Jeff's hurt expression, Sarah caught herself. "I'm sorry to snap like that. It's just the lack of sleep talking."

"Well, this guy seems to be getting you into a lot of trouble,"

Jeff persisted.

"He thinks the same thing about me."

Jeff gave her a perplexed look.

"Everybody is leaving me," Claude said out of the blue.

"We're not leaving you, Dad," Jeff replied soothingly. "I have to catch a flight around lunchtime, but Mom will stay with you all afternoon."

Sarah glared at her son.

"Lurlene lay on the bed beside me before she went in to work this morning," Claude crooned hopefully.

"Doing what?" Sarah inquired, realizing too late the unfortunate ambiguity of her question.

"She's a receptionist at Glidden Chiropractic in Chelsea," Claude replied, interpreting Sarah's question correctly, much to her relief.

There was a pause and Sarah announced, for no particular reason, "There was a car parked at the end of my driveway early this morning."

"It wasn't Lurlene," Claude said peevishly. "She's at work."

"Muffy said it was a man."

"What was he doing there?" Claude said.

"Watching my driveway, apparently. Muffy got his licence plate number."

"Gimme the number," Claude said.

"Dad—" Jeff protested.

"Gimme," Claude repeated, holding out his good hand.

Sarah rooted the slip of paper out of her purse and handed it to Claude.

"Cell phone," Claude demanded. "I won't have people stalking my wife in our own driveway."

"Ex-wife in *her* own driveway," Sarah corrected.

"Phone!"

"See what I mean about grouchy?" Jeff said, handing over his cell.

Claude laboriously punched in a number, using his good hand.

It was impressive, Sarah thought to herself with a smile, the number of useful people that lawyers, even tax attorneys, seemed to know.

After a brief conversation, Claude returned Jeff's cell and looked disapprovingly at Sarah.

"What are you," he demanded, "some kind of mobster magnet?"

"What are you talking about?"

"That car," Claude said portentously, "belongs to Anthony 'The Thumb' Demano, a Mafia Don. Did you know that?"

"You've got to be kidding. Of course not."

"You never mixed up with people like that when we were married," Claude whined. "Are you sure that boyfriend isn't involved with the Mafia?"

"For god's sake," She growled disgustedly.

Jeff had been fiddling with his cell, and he handed it to Sarah. "That's a file photo of Tony Demano I pulled from the Boston Globe. Look familiar?"

"I didn't see the man," she said. "I could ask Muffy, though. Still—" She squinted at the screen, pulled out her own cell, and called up her snapshot of the SOCC protesters in front of Ralph's house. Backing away from Claude's bed, she held the two phones side by side.

Jeff looked over her shoulder. "The pictures aren't too clear, but the man on your cell looks like a spitting image of Demano—the same long narrow face, dark eyes, hair, big ears—except twenty-five years younger."

"Demano's son?" Sarah said.

"What are you two whispering about?" Claude said.

"Nothing, Dad, we're just comparing some family photos." Lowering his voice, Jeff said, "Where did you take that picture?"

Sarah told him about the protesters.

"And your boyfriend took you there?"

"I wish you'd stop calling him 'my boyfriend' in that tone of voice. Besides, it was a friend of Oliver's who conned us into going there."

"What kind of a friend?"

"Stay out from under The Thumb's thumb," Claude murmured.

"Stop picking on my friends," Sarah hissed. "Why would the Mafia stake out my driveway, anyway?"

"Where's my cell?" Claude mumbled. "Got to call, find out how much to fix my Porsche."

"Dad, you don't have a Porsche any more. They had to jaws-of-life you out of the thing. It's in pieces. Little pieces."

"Little pieces?"

"Just because the car is registered to Demano doesn't mean he was in it," Sarah pointed out. "He probably has a dozen cars."

"So one of Demano's flunkies is casing your house?" Jeff said, trying to keep his voice low. "I don't like that any better, and what if the guy in your photo is Mafia too?"

Sarah glanced at Claude, who seemed to be asleep again. "An environmentalist mobster? Where's the money in that? This whole Mafia thing is ridiculous. Why in the world would they stake out my house? Anyway, I called the police and they're running extra cruisers down the road."

"I still don't think you should be in there alone," Jeff said stubbornly.

"You're worrying about nothing. I'll set the burglar alarm. The cops can be there in five minutes."

"A lot can happen in five minutes. I'm sure Muffy would be glad to put you up for a few days."

"That's my house, and I'm going to stay in it even if it is for sale, and the Realtor is going to tart it up! Dammit, I want a place of my own to live in! I'm fed up with living in other peoples' houses, and mooching off my friends!"

"Will you stop worrying about this mooching foolishness, and let people help?"

"I am staying in my house, and that's all there is to it," Sarah said threateningly.

"Do what your mom says, Jeff," Claude mumbled. "She's the boss. . . Lurlene is just a filly. . . Mom is the workhorse."

Jeff took a quick step to put himself between his semiconscious father and his mother's murderous advance.

"If we don't leave for the airport *right now*," Sarah snarled, "I will turn your father into turkeyburger."

"You need a vacation, Mom," Jeff said as he escorted her to the door. "But first, we need to figure out what to do with Dad."

"You're a sweet, and considerate child," she replied, taking his arm and patting it in a motherly fashion. "Ignorant as hell, but sweet."

Chapter 11

W hile Sarah was visiting Claude and worrying about where to live, Oliver was preparing to turn Pearly's cedar logs into boards.

Oliver's sawmill sat in a long, narrow open-sided shed behind his boatshop. From his position just to the right of the mill's five-foot blade he could see and hear it spinning with a faint humming, whistling sound and feel the light breeze of its teeth slicing the air.

Oliver cocked an ear at the ancient 6-cylinder industrial engine's throaty roar, eyed the blade to make sure it was running true, checked the log sitting on the carriage, and made sure that Eldon Tupper was standing at the far end of the mill, ready to off-load the first board.

Wes did not like the sawmill. The loud noises and strange, spinning things made him nervous, so he lay unhappily in a shady spot well apart from the mill, where he waited for his misguided master to slay the beast.

Eldon liked the sawmill for all the reasons that Wes disliked it. Quite aside from his attachment for noisy machinery, Eldon was here because cedar logs were heavy when they were this large, and his muscle would be needed.

The log lying on the mill's carriage was three-feet in diameter and twenty-feet long, the biggest of the batch.

Two posts on the back of the carriage held two spiked, horizontal arms, called "top dogs" that came down on top of the log to hold it in place. This being the first cut, the log was still round, and the top dogs were about all that kept the log from rolling into the blade and jamming it, with disastrous results.

For this reason, Oliver was especially cautious. Once the first slab was cut off, he and Eldon would rotate the log, putting the flat face down, and cut off the second slab, repeating the process until all four sides had flats and the log was ready to be cut into boards.

Oliver grasped the long control lever in front of him and tilted it slowly to the right, sending the carriage, with its log, trundling slowly down its track, like a miniature railroad flatcar, towards the waiting saw.

The first slab was thin, and the razor-sharp teeth sang as they effortlessly cut into the cedar, running straight and true, sending a stream of sawdust beneath the mill, where a blower shot it into a pile behind the shed.

The cut was almost finished, and Eldon was preparing to grab the slab as it came off the saw, when it happened.

In an instant, there was a thud, and the roar of the engine, the whine of the saw ceased, all motion frozen.

Oliver saw the huge log tilt at an impossible angle against the saw blade, and swore.

He turned to Eldon, standing some twenty feet away, and saw the fear etched into the young man's face.

"It's okay," Oliver assured him.

But for some reason Eldon was running towards him like a charging rhino, his mouth forming words that Oliver couldn't hear in the silence.

Oliver looked down, noticed his right hand pressed against his stomach, saw blood streaming between his fingers.

Eldon caught him as he fell.

Anthony The Thumb Demano enjoyed fine food, and he didn't allow that enjoyment to be marred by talking business while he ate. Because of this his nephew, Sal Demano, whose idea of fine dining meant a Big Mac and Fries, supersized, was forced to make small-talk while they consumed their hundred-dollar-a-plate luncheons.

As far as Sal's palate was concerned, they'd have been as well off eating at Papa Gino's—except for the Biscotti, which Sal liked a lot. He liked the wine too, though here again, a glass of three-dollar-a-bottle plonk would have suited him as well as the three-hundred-dollar stuff they were drinking.

At least he wasn't paying for all this.

This was the first time Sal had ever shared a meal—just him and Tony—and Sal knew it was a great honor, as well as a chance to prove himself, maybe get a leg up. This chance to eat with the Big Man could turn out to be well worth the drive down here to Boston.

"So," Tony said as he sipped his goblet of wine, the contents of which were worth enough to feed Sal a week's worth of lunches, "Tell me about the new guy who's running this SOCC group."

"He's dumb as a brick. The guy stages these protests and forgets to call the news people in time to get on TV. He was buffaloed by some bible-thumping truck driver during the last protest. If I hadn't been there, the whole thing would have fallen apart."

"Dumb can be useful," Tony commented, "and people with causes don't always think straight—makes them easy to manipulate, if you do it right."

Sal nodded his understanding. "At least he'll take a hint, and he's more in-your-face than Mueller was."

"I can see how Carl Mueller's death was maybe necessary," Tony mused, "but it was sloppily done, too risky. When we're established up there we'll have to run a tighter ship, and avoid taking chances like that."

Sal squirmed. "Nobody knew Mueller was going up there. I figured he was still looking at some other place."

"You've got to be careful with these idealists," Tony advised, "they're hard to predict." He sipped his wine pensively. "It's always good business to help an associate in need, Salvatore, and that's why I wanted you to work with those cedar people, but I'm disappointed with this associate. He's too impetuous, too unpredictable. We'll have to do better next year."

"Yeah, well a few weeks and I'll be out of there. And Carl's death does give us another lever. We'll just do things differently."

Tony nodded. "There's something else worries me. I don't like it that people are taking pictures of you, like you could end up in the evening news."

"I'm being careful. That thing with the woman taking my picture with her cell phone caught me by surprise."

"You can never be too careful with something like that," Tony commented. "I checked the tag numbers you gave me, and she lives out in Sudbury. Nice neighborhood. I sent Vinnie out for a look, and she's there all right."

Sal knew Vinnie Demano, another of Tony's nephews. The kid was barely twenty-five, street-tough, but not street-wise. Sal doubted if Vinnie could spot trouble if it came up and clipped him behind the ear. The Thumb obviously wasn't wasting a lot of talent on this woman, which suggested that he didn't think she was much of a threat, which also suggested that Tony didn't think Sal had screwed up too badly. It was a comforting conclusion.

"I wonder what she was doing in Maine," Sal mused.

"Her husband is a lawyer," The Thumb replied as he refilled their wine glasses.

"Too damn many lawyers in the world," Sal commented, trying to sound worldly.

"She's probably harmless," Tony said, "but I don't like the lawyer thing, so Vinnie's going to keep an eye on her for a while. Better safe than sorry."

Tony took another sip of wine. The way he was swilling the stuff, Sal figured they'd go through that three-hundred-dollar bottle in another ten minutes.

"Tell me about this wood-cutting business," Tony said, leaning back in his chair.

"They got some big timber-cutting operations up there," Sal replied, glad for the chance to show off his knowledge. "Did you know Maine is the most heavily forested state in the lower forty-eight? Surprised the hell out of me."

Tony nodded, smiling benignly at his protegee. "That's good Sal. It's big. Gives a guy with brains a lot of room to work. I like that."

"Of course, they don't have big trees like out west, like the redwood trees and all, but they've got a lot of them."

Sal paused to sip some of the wine, which was quite good, now that he thought about it. It was a rush to be explaining something to a man of The Thumb's stature.

"It's a big operation," Sal continued. "They got companies up there with big machines—million dollars worth of machines—just cutting down trees, Uncle Thumb—"

Sal knew he was in trouble the minute the words left his mouth.

Tony held up a forefinger to silence his nephew and leaned forward, his elbows on the embroidered linen tablecloth. "You know I don't like people calling me that, Salvatore."

"I'm sorry, Uncle Anthony," Sal babbled. "I just got carried away for a second." He was going to get The Lecture now for sure.

"Just because *maybe* I cut a guy's thumb off." Tony moved his finger back-and-forth like a windshield-wiper for emphasis. "Just because maybe I wanted to make a point, maybe teach this guy about respect—just for that one thing I maybe did, I gotta have people calling me The Thumb all the time."

Tony sighed. "It's a cross I'll bear, Salvatore, for the rest of my life."

"Yes, Uncle Anthony."

Tony smiled at Sal—a smile that didn't quite make it to his eyes. "It's okay, Sal. I'm just having some fun with you. But you know, I did the guy a favor. I taught him the importance of Respect. Respect and Loyalty. So it cost him a thumb, so what? It was a small price to learn about these things." Tony did the finger wagging thing again. "He's a better man for it today."

No matter how many times Sal heard the Thumb Lecture, he never ceased to feel uncomfortably aware of his own thumbs. What would it be like to have someone cut off your thumb? It would certainly hurt like hell, and then you'd go around with just one thumb for the rest of your life. It was rumored that the amputation had been done with a bolt cutter, which Tony kept in his garage should future instruction become necessary.

It was also rumored that Tony had gotten a taxidermist to mount the thumb on a key ring, like a rabbit's foot. Of course, that would have been some twenty, thirty years ago when Tony was Sal's age. He'd never seen Tony's key ring, and doubted that a stuffed thumb would last all that long in someone's pocket, anyhow.

Tony waggled his finger at Sal yet again. "You're a smart kid, Salvatore, but if you want to move up in the Organization you should never forget the principles of Respect and Loyalty."

Having completed The Lecture, Tony sat back. "So, tell me how this forestry thing works."

Sal knew what Tony was asking. He was asking about the money, about possible angles. Tony was considered a genius when it came to working angles, and Sal felt a thrill that he was being asked for input on something like this, showing that he had respect for Sal's knowledge.

Most important, it was an opportunity for Sal to open up a whole new area, get in on the ground floor of a brand new kind of operation. Sal was getting psyched.

"There are great possibilities, Uncle Tony. The way it works is the trucker picks up the logs and takes them to the mill. If they're big logs, they'll go to a sawmill. If they're small, they'll probably go to a paper mill. Even the branches and brush get chipped up and trucked away."

Tony was beginning to look a little bored, so Sal hurried on. "Anyhow, all the money gets cut up between the trucker, the loggers, and the landowner."

The Thumb sipped his wine, thinking. "Yeah," he said appreciatively, "I like it. Lots of money going through lots of hands. All those cuts. A smart guy could make some dough working a sideline like that, and trucking is something we know about."

"And SOCC is in the right place to work some of those angles, squeeze a little here and there," Sal added.

Tony nodded again. This time, the smile went all the way to his eyes.

"SOCC is starting to get a rep, Uncle Tony. People are learning to step aside when they see us coming, 'cause they know we can give them big trouble—all those lawyers taking them to court. And the beauty is that it's all legit. We play our cards right and SOCC will be all over the state before you know it."

"Just don't go too far too fast," Tony cautioned. "Work one angle at a time. Slow and sure beats fast and sloppy every time. Young people can be impatient and end up getting into trouble."

Tony finished his wine and stared at the nearly empty bottle.

"You got to use your brain, and you got to use your smarts. You know what I mean?"

"I think so, Uncle Tony," Sal assured him, pleased that The Thumb obviously had enough confidence in his ability to give him a free reign, even if it came with fatherly advice attached. "We need to make sure this first operation works smooth before we try something more. One step at a time. We learn how things are done now, and make our move next year."

Tony nodded, raising a cautionary finger. "Always go slow, and know what you're doing before you eliminate an associate, even if he is just a middleman."

"Yes, Uncle Tony."

"Remember we're business people now," The Thumb cautioned. "When I say 'eliminate' I don't mean like the old days, when people got killed all the time. Today, if somebody comes to us with a problem he wants us to help him with, we maybe find out that the guy is a little short, maybe he's lost money gambling, and certain people are getting upset with him because he can't pay up. Being business people, we help solve his problem, help him with his debts, so now he owes us."

"So then we can buy this middleman out, and now we're in charge, and everybody is happy," Sal concluded, "especially where this person has been a pain in the ass."

Tony paused, nodded in agreement. "You've got what it takes to go far in the Organization, Salvatore," he said. "You do good on a job like this and you can move right up into some of the big stuff."

Sal, who had thought he was already working on some big stuff, smiled and decided the fancy food and the three-hundred-dollar-a-bottle wine were pretty good after all.

What the hell happened?" Pearly said as he entered the hospital waiting area and sat beside Eldon.

"I'm not sure. We were sawing that big log, everything fine, then there was this bang, the log jammed up on the saw, and the next thing I know, Oliver was standing there bleeding like a stuck pig."

"Splinter off the log?"

"Maybe. The slab we were cutting was thin and it did kind of shatter. I didn't have time to look around, though. Jesus, I never saw so much blood," Eldon said, his voice shaky at the memory. "Didn't think he was going to make it."

Pearly had seen more than his share of blood during a tour in Vietnam, so he could sympathize with his companion. "He'll be fine once they sew him up," he said, resting a hand on Eldon's massive shoulder.

The pair of them ended up having to sit in the waiting area for almost three hours before a doctor in blue scrubs turned up.

"You the person who called 911?" he said to Eldon.

"Yes."

"You ever had first-aid training?"

"I was trained as an EMT," Eldon replied. "Never did anything with it, though."

The doctor looked at Eldon gravely. "You never did anything with it? You saved a man's live with it today. It's a damn good thing you were there and acted quickly."

"I was lucky," Eldon demurred.

"So was your friend."

"How is he?" Pearly said.

"Lacerated the small intestine in three places and nicked an artery," the doctor replied. "An inch further over and he never would have made it to the hospital in time. There was internal bleeding, a lot of blood loss. We stitched everything up and cleaned out the area as best we could, but some debris got carried into the wound, so he'll be on IV antibiotics for a while until we're sure there's no infection in there."

"This is what we dug out of him." The doctor held out a clear plastic container, which looked to Eldon like a Petri dish from his college biology class. "What the hell is it?" the doctor asked.

Eldon took the dish and looked at its contents. "It's a saw tooth."

"That would do it," Pearly muttered.

"Saw tooth? It looks like an oversized human incisor."

Eldon removed the lid and took out the tooth. It did look sort of like a giant tooth, he thought, with a razor-sharp edge curving out wickedly from its root.

"A sawmill blade is almost five feet around and cost two-grand or more," Pearly explained. "You don't want to buy a new one just because the teeth get worn or nicked, so they make the teeth removable. That way you can replace them."

"Do they come off very often?" the doctor asked.

"Hell, no. They've got a cam-like thing to hold them in. Uses a special wrench. Those things don't come off without a damn good reason."

Eldon examined the tooth while Pearly talked, and noticed the cutting edge was still sharp, but the inside face of the forged steel was scraped and dented.

Eldon handed the container to Pearly, shooting him a look.

Pearly studied the tooth for a moment, nodded, and returned it to the doctor.

"Keep that safe," Pearly said. "Oliver will want to see it when he wakes up."

"Don't worry, I'll leave it at the nurse's station. They'll make sure he gets it."

"How long before we can see him?" Eldon said, suddenly impatient.

"He'll be in Recovery for a while before they transfer him to a room. You should be able to talk to him in a couple of hours."

"That'll give me time to go and take care of Wes," Eldon said.

"Who is Wes?" the doctor asked.

"Oliver's dog. I just threw him in the house when the ambulance arrived. He was pretty upset."

"I'll go with you," Pearly said.

The doctor nodded. "Look, your friend will be here for a few days. We put in a couple of drains, and he won't be leaving until they're clear. Like I said, there was a lot of dirt and a fragment of his shirt embedded in the wound, so I can't take a chance of any infection getting by us. Plus, he's lost a lot of blood, so it'll be a while before he gets his strength back."

Having smelled Oliver's blood and seen the ambulance roaring up the driveway with its siren blaring, Wes had been understandably upset when Eldon unceremoniously shut him in the house.

The dog shot out the door when Pearly and Eldon opened it, dashed around to the back of the shop, and began pawing at the patch of blood on the ground, whining as he did so.

Wes growled when Eldon pulled him a way from the stained dirt while Pearly covered the spot with fresh sawdust, and it took several minutes of patting and soothing before Wes was willing to lie down and watch the two men work.

Cedar is a fairly light-weight wood, but even so, it took both of them, and a pair of Peaveys, to lever the big log back onto the sawmill carriage.

Eldon poked at the bark with his pocket knife while Pearly examined the saw blade. The way the log had jammed it, he figured the blade was going to need some work before it would run true again.

"Jesus," Eldon said after a moment. "There's a nail in there."

"So what? That saw would cut through a nail, no problem. Dull it up some, but it sure wouldn't pull out a tooth."

Eldon dug some more with his knife. "This ain't an ordinary nail; it's a damn big spike." Eldon turned to Pearly. "Somebody must have driven the spike in, then used a punch of some kind to drive it below the bark so nobody would notice it. The saw must have hit it just right, the tooth popped out, ricocheted off something, and got Oliver. Freak accident."

"Freak accident, hell. You're saying the tree's been spiked." Pearly swore vehemently. "If there's one spike, there's probably a dozen in there."

Eldon clambered onto the carriage to poke at the log with his knife. "Cedar bark is so furry, it's hard to find anything—" He paused, working with the knife-tip. "Wait, feels like there's something under the bark here. . . Yeah, another spike."

Pearly was livid now, swearing and kicking at the ground like an enraged bull.

Wes came over and stood uncertainly beside Pearly, whining worriedly.

"Every one of these goddam logs may be spiked," Pearly snarled, among a string of epithets. "The whole load is worthless."

"We can get a metal detector and pull them out. Hate to waste such nice logs," Eldon replied. He'd found a third spike, but decided not to mention it. It looked as though somebody had driven a ring of them around the trunk, about three feet up from the base of the tree.

"I don't want anyone else getting hurt sawing on these damn things. It's a good thing Jack Fournier didn't hit a spike with his chain saw."

"I didn't think people spiked trees anymore," Eldon said. "I thought that went out thirty years ago." He thought there might be a fourth spike, but it was pretty much underneath the log where he couldn't get at it well enough to be sure. "These haven't been here very long; there's hardly any rust on them."

"Are you sure?"

"Can't have been more than a few months."

Pearly stopped swearing and gazed at the logs—logs he'd paid good money for, and could turn out to be riddled with spikes.

"I've heard where a group of people used to get together to spike trees. Drive some in around the base, put up a ladder and drive another bunch eight or ten feet up. But nobody has done that kind of thing for years."

"It's a hell of a lot of work, driving a bunch of spikes like that into a tree," Eldon commented, echoing Pearly's somber thoughts.

"I think we'd better get some tools out of Oliver's shop," Pearly said, "so we can pull out one of those bastards and look at it."

_____

Chapter 13

Sarah knew that Lurlene would be visiting Claude later in the afternoon, so she picked up a late lunch after dropping Jeff off at Logan airport and drove home.

She had convinced herself that the stranger in her driveway was just a coincidence—someone parking to consult a map or make a phone call—not really a threat.

After all, why would a mobster with a name like Tony The Thumb care about her? Unless, of course, he was thinking about buying her house and wanted to get a feel for the neighborhood. The man might be looking for a little peace and quiet after a busy day of thuggery, so naturally he would want to see how much traffic went by.

Perhaps he was on the way over this very minute with a suitcase full of money to pay for the place.

In spite of these happy fantasies, Sarah made sure the doors and windows were locked and the alarm activated, though she resented feeling like a prisoner in the only house she had.

The ever vigilant Muffy was at the door within minutes of Sarah's arrival.

"I just popped in for a second to see if you'd like to come over for supper," Muffy said. "Gary is away on business, so the two of us can have a nice girl-meal, a little wine, and lots of gossip."

"That sounds great," Sarah said enthusiastically. "I have to make some phone calls first, but I'll be over in a couple of hours."

"I'll be ready. How is Claude doing?"

"He seems okay."

"You don't sound very sure," Muffy said, looking at Sarah quizzically.

"It's probably just the trauma, but he's spends a lot of time sleeping. He'll wake up and be alert for a while, and then he kind of fades out."

"That's just the head injury," Muffy pronounced. "I've read they can be tricky. Do the doctors have any idea when he can be released?"

"Not yet. They have him standing up and shuffling around the room as best he can on one leg, but that's about it so far."

"What in the world are you going to do with him when he gets out?"

"I'm working on it," Sarah replied in a tone of voice that lifted Muffy's eyebrows a notch.

"And you won't have him here."

"I've already told you that I have no intention of being my ex-husband's caretaker and landlord, as well as mother to his ditzy child lover."

"I can see your point," Muffy said, nodding, "but still—"

"Besides," Sarah interrupted, "I'm trying to sell this place, and the Realtor wants to stage the house. I'm not even sure she'll let *me* live here."

Muffy looked around. "It looks pretty tidy now. What's the Realtor's problem?"

"It damn well should look tidy, considering the number of times the house-cleaning service has been in here over the summer," Sarah grumbled. "The Realtor wants to bring in some different furniture, some flower arrangements, and god knows what else to dress the place up."

"Oh," Muffy said in a small voice.

"It won't even feel like my house by the time she's done," Sarah said plaintively, fighting back tears. "It'll be the Realtor's place. I don't know where I'm going to live anymore."

Muffy, normally the ultimate hard-headed pragmatist, took Sarah in her arms. "It will all work out in time, dear. Meanwhile, I'm going to make us a nice meal of comfort food. Lots of chocolate," she promised.

———

Sarah was just getting ready to go over to Muffy's house later that afternoon when her cell chimed.

"I've been trying to reach you all afternoon," Pearly said brusquely, "but your line's been busy."

"I've been on the phone most of the afternoon."

"I called Kate, and she said you'd gone off to Boston, something about your ex-husband having a car accident. Hope he's okay."

"Claude's doing better. Broken leg, broken arm, and a head injury."

"In that little red car of his?" Pearly said in a tone of voice that made it clear he couldn't imagine anybody surviving a crash in Claude's Porsche.

"Yes."

"That's a tough break. Hope he'll be back on his feet soon."

"Not likely. At least for a while," Sarah replied, torn between impatience and curiosity about what Pearly had on his mind.

"Thought you'd like to know that Oliver had sort of an accident with his sawmill this morning and is in the hospital."

Sarah sat down abruptly. "What kind of an accident?" she said, her mind swirling with grisly possibilities.

"A sawtooth came off, caught him in the stomach," Pearly said matter-of-factly. "He got out of surgery four hours ago. They think they got everything patched up inside, but he lost a lot of blood."

Why was it, Sarah wondered peevishly, that the two men in her life had to end up in the hospital at the same time. Life just didn't seem fair.

"A sawtooth came off?" she said numbly, sensing there was worse to come.

"It didn't come off by accident."

"I though you just said it *was* an accident."

"I said 'sort of' an accident," Pearly corrected her.

"I've had a long day, Gaites," she snapped. "Are you going to tell me what the hell is going on, or do I have to drag it out of you a bit at a time?"

Pearly filled her in on the day's events.

"Nobody seems to know who spiked the trees, but the cops are investigating," he concluded.

Sarah vaguely remembered news stories about trees being spiked years ago, but that was out on the west coast. "I didn't think people did that kind of thing anymore."

"They haven't for years, that I know of. Not until now, anyway. It'll probably be in the news," he concluded.

"In the news?"

"Somebody must have tipped them off. A couple of reporters turned up at the hospital a few minutes ago. It'll be on the local channels for sure, and maybe even CNN."

"Oh, hell."

"Don't worry. Nobody's going to let them talk to Oliver until he's good and ready," Pearly reassured her. "I can give you Oliver's number at the hospital, if you want to call him—"

"Of course I want to call him, dammit!"

There was a hurt silence on the line.

"I'm sorry, Pearly. It's just that everything is landing on me at once."

"Yeah, I know how that is. I was just going to say it would be better to wait until tomorrow morning. He's pretty much out of it right now."

———————

Sarah didn't sleep well that night.

At one point she dreamed of ancient cellar holes, foundation stones tumbled, the buried debris of long-ago lives moldering away in dark corners, the shattered, rotting remains of beloved family furniture, the gay toys of childhood buried and rusting in the dirt, skeletons in the ashes, all of it covered over with dead leaves and rotting lilac blossoms.

And somewhere under the cold soil, she lay suffocating, clawing for air.

Sarah awoke with a start in the wee-small hours, soaked with sweat, worried that she was losing her mind, and wondering what cellar holes meant to her subconscious brain.

Once again, she feared that the summer was catching up with her at last.

Sarah was up before dawn, pacing through the silent house, looking at the forlorn books, furniture, and clothing she had left behind when she went to Maine last May. Everything looked gray and indistinct, almost unreal, in the pre-dawn light.

The house was cool, but Sarah put on a jacket, rather than turn up the furnace. It seemed more appropriate, somehow, as though it was already someone else's furnace.

As she wandered aimlessly from room to room, Sarah wondered where she was going to live. Claude had been generous with the divorce settlement, so money wasn't a major issue in the decision of where to live, but where was home? Was it here, or in Maine?

How different the last few months in Maine had been, compared to the idyllic summers of her youth at Burnt Cove's Camp Migawoc. The place had been run like a big, boisterous family back then, with Kate and Sam Merlew as the benevolent if sometimes overly permissive parents.

Sarah's parents had scrimped and saved to pay for her summers at Migawoc—where many of her fellow campers were from much wealthier families—and her return home in the fall to her close-knit blue-collar family had meant a period of readjustment.

Two carefree lives, Burnt Cove and Boston, two cultures, neatly separated, with no need to chose one or the other. But her parents were both gone now, along with her youth, and the choices that lay ahead were hers alone.

In the pre-dawn stillness, Sarah heard a car passing by, driving slowly.

She thought about calling Oliver, but it wasn't quite four o'clock yet, early, even by hospital time, and she was afraid that hearing his voice would pull her away from her responsibilities here.

If she could only figure out what her responsibilities were.

Sarah meandered through the diningroom towards the front of the house. The Realtor had talked about bringing in "more imposing" furnishings for the front hall, in order to make a "good first impression" on prospective buyers. What was wrong with the impression her house made now?

A man was standing in the front hall.

Sarah got a glimpse of a dark sweatshirt, black jeans—a form in the dimness.

The room spun as she fell, landed hard, stunned and winded.

He stood over her for a second, tall, menacing, as though unsure what to do.

Then he was gone, leaving the front door ajar.

———————

The two uniformed policemen spent almost an hour walking through the house with Sarah. Finally, they returned to the front hall.

One of the policemen was tall, with a long, hound-dog face, while the other was short and a little chubby, with a round, cheerful face. Sarah couldn't help thinking of them as Abbott and Costello after the comic duo—not that there was anything comical about them, or the situation.

"So, all he took was your purse?" Abbott said.

"I can't see anything else missing."

"You must have scared him off before he could snatch anything more," Costello said. "If it's any comfort, you probably scared him as much as he scared you. The last thing a burglar wants is to find somebody home."

Abbott looked at his notes. "Let me verify this: you were walking around the house in the dark and bumped into him in the front hall?"

"It wasn't completely dark, and I was having trouble sleeping, so I was walking around a little."

"With the lights off."

"I told you that," Sarah said, irritated by Abbott's apparent scepticism.

"I'm not doubting what you said, just trying to make sure we have it straight."

"It explains why you caught him by surprise, you see," Costello added soothingly. "He'd have taken off for sure if he knew you were up."

"And all you could tell about him is that he was tall and slender, and was wearing dark clothing?" Abbott said.

"It all happened so fast, and there wasn't much light. He knocked me down and was gone out the door almost before I realized he was there."

"The guy was a pro," Costello said. "You were lucky. An amateur might have panicked and hurt you."

"We can have someone come over and check for prints, but my guess is he was too smart to leave any."

"I had the alarm set," Sarah said. "How did he get in?"

"It was a second-storey job," Costello said. "Cat burglar."

"Your alarm system is pretty old, and it just covers the ground floor doors and windows," Abbott added. "It looks like he used one of your trash barrels to get onto the garage roof and then jimmied the second floor window. Took him two minutes, tops. Some of those guys are regular monkeys."

Costello looked at her sympathetically. "Be a good idea for you to upgrade your system—add protection to the upstairs, put in some motion detectors, outside lighting."

"You still look pretty shaky, Ms. Cassidy," Abbott said. "We could have the EMTs here in a New York minute, make sure you're okay."

"Be a good idea," Costello said, "just to be on the safe side. Sometimes, a person can get banged up worse than he realizes—"

"I'm fine, really," Sarah replied, "and I have a friend right across the street."

"You want us to take you over?"

"I expect she'll come over here."

Costello nodded with a smile. "Woke her up with all the blinking lights, you think?"

"I'm sure of it."

Abbott handed here some papers. "Here's something we hand out. It's a checklist of things you should do about you credit cards, checking accounts, cell phone carriers—things you'll need to do to protect yourself."

"I suppose this happens a lot," Sarah said, suddenly feeling exhausted.

"A hell of a lot more than it should," Costello replied sadly.

"I'll never see my purse again, will I?"

Abbott looked at her, his bloodhound face solemn. "It would be a miracle," he said.

Chapter 14

W hile Sarah was dealing with the Sudbury police, Bruce Nash, proprietor of Arden Forest Services, was confronting a Maine State Police trooper.

"What do you mean, people are spiking trees on this woodlot? Who the hell does that anymore?" Bruce demanded. He was wearing a navy blue hoodie against the chill dawn air. The cuffs were frayed, and a grease stain marred the "Arden Forest Services" logo.

"A sawmill operator was severely injured yesterday by a spiked log," the trooper replied.

"The only logs that have been taken off this lot are the cedars Jack Fournier cut," Bruce said, swearing. "You should talk to those Save Our Cedars Coalition wing-nuts. We've had trouble with them in the past."

"Do you know for a fact that they've spiked trees in the past, Mr. Nash?"

"No," Bruce admitted, "but I wouldn't put it past them. They've made trouble every other way with their arguing over timber cutting permits, and getting judges to issue crazy restraining orders, and all the damn-fool picketing they're doing."

"We'll look into it," the trooper assured him.

"So when can we get in there and start cutting?"

"As soon as we finish our investigation."

"What's to investigate? I'll just send in my crew with metal detectors, and they can mark any spiked trees. That way, you can investigate the hell out of them before we cut them down."

"You can cut all you want *after* we finish our investigation."

"When the hell is that going to happen? Jesus, I've got a crew coming in at seven o'clock! Do you expect me to send them home with no work and no pay? Do you know how much it costs to have all that machinery standing idle?"

"Your crew will have to wait," the trooper said, with labored patience. "A man was murdered in here four days ago, and now we learn that trees have been spiked nearby. The two things may very well be related, in which case those trees are a part of a murder investigation. We take murder very seriously, Mr. Nash."

Bruce heaved a sigh. "Look, there's two square *miles* of woods in here. Are you going to investigate *all* of it?"

"I doubt that we'll go anywhere near that far, but we will go where the evidence leads us."

———

It was time for breakfast and Sal was hungry. Yesterday's lunch with Tony had reminded him of how much he missed Boston. He wished he was back in the North End where he'd grown up with his friends instead of being stuck in this damned motel in Augusta, Maine. At least in Boston he'd be able to keep an eye on Vinnie, maybe knock his head against the wall a few times—discretely, of course, where Vinnie was The Thumb's nephew. As far as Sal could see, Tony was too soft-hearted when it came to his relatives, thumb or no thumb.

Just because Vinnie was the son of Tony's kid brother didn't mean he was smart.

"You actually broke into the Cassidy woman's house and mugged her?" Sal said incredulously, glaring into his cell, as though trying to give Vinnie a long-distance evil eye.

"I didn't mug her for chrissake. She was walking around in the dark in the middle of the night—scared me half to death. I thought she was a ghost or something. I bumped into her, knocked her down on the way out the door, that's all."

"Did Tony tell you to break into her house?"

"Well, not exactly," Vinnie replied nervously, "but he told me to keep an eye on her, see what she was up to."

Sal heaved a sigh. "Keeping an eye on her does not mean breaking into her house and getting caught at it. The Thumb is going to be pissed at you, Vinnie."

"Come on, Sal, I'm a second-storey man. That's what I do. If Tony didn't want the broad's house burglarized, why did put me on the job?"

"Damned if I know why he did that," Sal replied. "All I know is you're in a deep hole."

"He doesn't have to learn about it, does he?" Vinnie pleaded.

"Are you kidding? I couldn't keep it a secret if I tried. The Thumb knows everything, probably already knows you broke in. If Cassidy went to the cops and reported it, Tony has already read the report. Trust me on this, you're going to hear from him."

"I did get some good information," Vinnie said hopefully. "That should help."

A vice tightened on Sal's chest. "What did you do?"

"I lifted her purse. It was right on the hall table."

"You took her purse," Sal said flatly. "And where is it now?"

Vinnie paused. "In the trunk of the car."

"*Tony's* car? The purse, with your prints all over it, is in Tony's

Buick?"

"I'll get rid of it as soon as I hang up," Vinnie gabbled.

"You'd better get rid of it quick, before Tony gets rid of you."

"She had her cell phone in the purse," Vinnie said enticingly.

"You didn't turn it on, did you?"

"Just for a minute or two, while I was driving," Vinnie assured Sal.

"Okay," Sal said dubiously, "so what was on it?"

"A picture of you with those SOCC picketers. I bet The Thumb won't be happy to see that," Vinnie replied triumphantly.

"He already knows about the picture, Vinnie. That's why you're checking up on Cassidy, remember?"

"Okay, right," Vinnie said, deflated. "But there's also a couple of pictures of some logging machinery—at least that's what it looks like. It says 'Arden Forest Services' on one of them."

That brought Sal up short. "Recent pictures?"

"Date stamp says Tuesday."

So Cassidy had not only visited Ralph Barnes, she'd also visited the woodlot on the same day. Sal began to think Vinnie's break-in hadn't been such a bad idea after all. What was the woman up to?

"What else have you got?" Sal asked.

"A bunch of phone numbers. One of them is for the nursing home where they've got Derwin Denton in Yarmouth, Maine."

Sal was impressed. Vinnie might be smarter than he seemed.

The trouble was, now Sal was getting worried about what kind of problems Cassidy might make for him. "That's good information, Vinnie," he said. "You may not loose your thumb after all."

"You put in a good word with Tony for me?" Vinnie said hopefully.

"Sure, but for chrissake, be more careful next time. And make sure you destroy the phone so nobody can trace it. I mean beat it with a hammer, throw it in the fire, make sure there's nothing left for the cops to find. And get rid of that damn purse."

Sal figured he'd better start being more careful too. Of course it was possible that Cassidy just happened to be a friend of Ralph Barnes, and she had a thing for woodlots and timber harvesting machinery, but why take any chances? Sal began to feel better about having Vinnie on the job. Between Mueller's murder, and now Cassidy, things could get complicated fast.

———

Having had the foresight to warm up her Audi as soon as she saw the police car pull into her neighbor's driveway, Muffy descended on Sarah like an animated security blanket within seconds of the cruiser's departure. Muffy was unstoppable in her mothering mode, and Sarah was bundled into the Audi's cozy warmth, driven across the street, seated at Muffy's kitchen table, and dosed with herb tea before Sarah had a chance to protest.

As a result of her friend's ministrations, Sarah didn't get a chance to call Oliver as she had planned. This was probably a good thing since he was busy entertaining guests in his hospital room.

———

Oliver had been in the hospital for less than twenty-four hours and he was feeling sore, weak, bored, irritable, but above all, frustrated that nobody was willing to tell him when he could go home.

Pearly, full of good cheer, appeared in Oliver's room on the dot of 9:00 a.m. with a stranger.

"They feed you well in this place?" Pearly inquired.

"They're promising pablum this afternoon," Oliver replied gloomily.

"Bet you can't wait."

"Bug off."

Pearly suppressed a smile and introduced his companion as Dan Finlon.

"Jack gave me his name," Pearly said, "because he's worked with Dan before, and Dan is the forester who's working on Denton's woodlot, and just about every other woodlot around there. Anyway, he's an expert on spiking trees."

"I'm not really an expert," Dan said modestly. "I do know that back in the eighties and nineties certain radical conservation groups used to spike trees as a way to discourage lumber companies from cutting an old-growth forest, but I haven't heard of anybody doing that kind of thing for years. Certainly not in this part of Maine." Dan shook his head sadly. "I can't imagine why anybody would spike trees nowadays. I feel guilty for not having noticed the spikes when I marked the trees."

"They were driven in below the bark, so they were pretty hard to see," Pearly said as he handed Dan one of the spikes which he and Eldon had extracted.

"Looks like somebody really meant business," Dan commented as he studied the ten-inch-long spike. "Lot of work to drive that in below the bark so people like me wouldn't notice it," he added ruefully.

"I don't understand," Oliver said. "I thought the whole point of spiking trees was to stop anybody from cutting them down."

"It is," Dan replied, "but you also don't want to make it too easy to find the spikes, or remove them."

"Sure," Oliver replied, "but what I'm getting at is why didn't the tree spiker, or spikers, tell anybody about it? Isn't that the whole point—to let everyone know the trees are spiked so they won't be cut down?"

"Maybe they didn't want to get arrested for trespass and destruction of property," Pearly suggested.

"Back when this sort of thing was going on," Dan explained, "the Earth Liberation Front, or ELF, used to advertise in the papers that a piece of forest had been spiked. Of course, it's almost impossible for the law to prosecute vandalism like that, unless they're caught red-handed."

"But nobody has told anyone about these trees being spiked," Oliver persisted. "Why not?"

"Maybe they didn't have time," Dan replied. "Maybe they didn't know Jack Fournier was going in there so soon to cut those cedars. Maybe they weren't finished spiking the trees. The fact is that spiking trees never did work. If the loggers knew a stand of trees had been spiked, they and the mills would just use metal detectors to find and remove them."

Dan placed the spike on Oliver's bedside table. "Of course it slowed the logging process down to do that, and you might miss a spike or two if you weren't careful. The real trouble was that the people who got hurt were the loggers and the mill operators."

"Like Oliver," Pearly commented.

Dan nodded. "The landowners weren't the ones being sliced with broken saw chains or saw teeth, so it didn't discourage them from having their land cut off. That was the flaw, and that was why the activists eventually disavowed tree-spiking. It wasn't accomplishing what they wanted and the wrong people were getting hurt."

"Was it just Pearly's cedars that were spiked?" Oliver asked.

"Bruce Nash is planning to go over the area with a metal detector to get some idea of how many others there are," Dan replied.

"It'll take a helluva long time to go over the whole woodlot," Pearly said.

"Yes it will," Dan agreed, "but they'll probably just have to check the bigger trees."

"SOCC is the logical candidate to have spiked the cedars," Oliver said.

"Unless they were framed, like Ralph," Pearly commented.

"Maybe it isn't just the cedars that were spiked," Oliver suggested.

"Very possible," Dan agreed. "Those cedars just happened to be the first trees that were cut."

"I'd love to get my hands on whoever did it," Oliver growled.

"I'm no fan of SOCC," Dan said. "They've given me a lot of grief in the last few years. And they've made plenty of other enemies too. On the other hand, I can't see Carl Mueller spiking trees—he was too smart to risk the bad publicity." Dan paused. "But I'm not so sure about Ken Poirier."

"Why not?" Oliver asked. "Why would he invite bad publicity?"

Dan thought for a moment, choosing his words carefully. "The guy's erratic. He's very ambitious, has dreams of making SOCC a major force all across the state, instead of just a small, regional group of flakes, like it is now. For him, any kind of publicity is good, so long as it attracts new members."

"So he's going after the angry, lunatic fringe?" Pearly suggested.

"If you ask me, the whole organization is a bunch of con artists and flakes," Dan replied. "The Maine Forest Service ranks cedar as a category S4, or 'apparently secure,' in the state. SOCC will tell you that 'apparently secure' is only one step up from S3, meaning 'rare,' but that's just semantics. The fact is that there's no real shortage of cedar in Maine, no matter what SOCC says. Sure, there aren't many really big trees left around this part of the state, like the ones you got, but Northern White Cedar doesn't usually grow that big in Maine anyway. Those clowns are trying to create a crisis where there isn't one, though I suppose there are enough gullible people out there willing to donate to the cause. And as for Denton's property, there's only that one stand of cedar on the entire place."

"Then why the hell is SOCC bothering with them?" Pearly said.

Dan shrugged. "Like I say, all I know is that Ken Pourier is unpredictable as hell, and he probably sees a chance to get some publicity up there."

Just then, a nurse rushed into the room. "Quick, you're in the news," she told Oliver, grabbing the TV remote from the bedside table.

"I was afraid of this," Pearly muttered.

They had missed the first part of the news item, but they learned that the unidentified sawmill operator survived emergency surgery and was expected to live.

"I'm glad to hear that," Oliver commented.

"Hush," Pearly hissed. "Here's that guy who was picketing Ralph's place."

"Ken Pourier, the sonofabitch who's running SOCC," Dan said.

Ken was staring into the lens with a nervousness he was unable to hide behind a facade of outrage. "As the leader of the Save Our Cedars Coalition, I can assure you that our organization deplores this despicable action, this cowardly act of terrorism in our forest. SOCC has never engaged in this sort of vandalism and we disavow such actions. I can assure you that our organization is dedicated to protecting the cedar trees of our great state through legal means, by passing appropriate legislation and by ensuring the laws we have in place are strictly enforced."

"Hypocritical bastard," Dan muttered.

Chapter 15

Claude was dozing in his bed with the TV on and the volume set low when Sarah arrived around noon. She briefly thought about waking him, but decided it would be more peaceful to just sit quietly for a while.

She had spent the morning cancelling her credit cards, closing her checking account, and working down the check list Abbott and Costello had given her. It was barely lunchtime, and the day already felt far too long.

The TV jolted her back to the present. She leaned forward, fingering the remote to raise the volume.

The news media, bored with the usual tales of terrorism, wars, and political gridlock, and eager to cover something different, had given lavish coverage to SOCC and the spiked cedar tree.

The news-hounds had discovered Oliver's name and reported it gleefully, along with his medical diagnosis, before airing Ken Pourier's indignant denials.

"Isn't that your boyfriend they're talking about?" Claude said, startling Sarah.

"I thought you were asleep," she replied, realizing with a shock that she still hadn't called Oliver.

"He's in the hospital."

"Yes."

"Like me."

"Not quite," she said. "He'll probably be out in a day or two, way before you are."

"Have you called him?"

"Not yet, Claude. I've had a really bad morning. Someone broke into my—"

"Why are you here?" he interrupted, sounding upset.

"What?"

Claude shifted uneasily in the bed. "You should be there, with him."

"And who is going to take care of you? Lurlene?"

"I don't care. You should be there with him, not your ex-husband." Claude shifted again, looking agitated.

Sarah sat, stunned. This wasn't the Claude she was used to, the man who had spent the summer trying to lure her back. "That's sweet of you, Claude," she managed.

"Only fair to let you go."

"As a matter of fact, I was thinking of going up tomorrow, for a day, maybe two."

"Not fair to keep you here. Time for you to move on." He paused. "Hurts."

"Yes. Divorces hurt," she said softly.

"Hurts," he repeated.

Sarah lurched to her feet, her eyes darting to Claude's face as she reached for the nurse's call button.

It was only a few precious minutes—though the time seemed much longer—before Claude was being rushed down the corridor, amid a flurry of nurses and urgent pages over the speaker system.

———————

"You know, Salvatore, that I don't like to look over anybody's shoulder," Tony said. "I give somebody a job, it's because I trust them to do it right."

"Yes, Uncle Anthony," Sal replied. He'd been dreading this call all day.

"But I'm hearing things. And these things, they worry me, you know what I'm talking about?"

"Yes, Uncle Anthony."

"This tree spiking thing."

"Yes, Uncle Anthony."

"You know that I don't want to hear any details on the phone right now—you understand what I'm saying, Salvatore."

"Yes, Uncle Anthony." Tony was saying that the feds had a permanent bug on his phone.

"I don't care if this organization you're working with, these SOCC people, had anything to do this spiking business."

"Yes, Uncle Anthony."

"The thing is, it looks bad. It's the wrong kind of publicity—"

"Yes, Uncle Anthony."

"—even if they didn't have anything to do with it."

"SOCC has gotten an awful lot of new donations since the news got out," Sal commented.

"But it's the wrong kind of money. It's tainted money. We have to be careful to uphold our standards, Salvatore, or we'll have no respect. And without respect, a person is nothing."

Sal didn't see why taking money from idiots who thought spiking trees was a good idea could be any worse than some of the things Tony did, but then he wasn't a genius capo like The Thumb, who was always a step ahead when it came to figuring angles.

"Like I said before," Sal replied, "Ken isn't smart. He might have done something dumb like that."

"It sounds like maybe SOCC would be better off with a new head," Tony said in his gentlest, most fatherly voice. "I hate to see you working with all these careless associates. They make needless trouble for everybody."

Sal's blood ran cold. "I'll keep on the situation," he promised.

"The other thing, Salvatore. Our woman friend seems pretty smart."

"Yes, Uncle Anthony."

"Vinnie gave me an update on the situation with her—"

Situation? Sal didn't like the sound of that word. It had the feel of trouble. Trouble for him.

"—and I think we should keep in touch with her for a while longer, but discretely."

"Vinnie isn't always very discrete," Sal commented carefully.

"I've talked to him about that. He's young still, and too eager sometimes," Tony said. "Be patient with him."

"Yes, Uncle Anthony."

"You're doing a good job, Salvatore, but I want you to be careful. Don't overreach. Keep a low profile."

———

Being a large, some might say huge, and amiable young man with a wide range of acquaintances, Eldon Tupper had an edge when it came to scrounging things. He had exploited this talent to cadge a metal detector of the type designed for use on trees. He spent almost an hour clambering over the cedar logs on the brow of Oliver's sawmill, scouring every inch of wood in search of more spikes.

Except for a ring of spikes girdling the one log that had brought Oliver such grief, there were no other spikes, nails, scraps of barbed wire fence, or any other metallic objects embedded in the logs.

It made no sense.

Eldon sat on one of the logs, scratched Wes behind the ears, and wondered what was going on. Why drive spikes in just one tree? Jack Fournier had told Pearly that the cedars were all in a single, small area, so why stop with just one? Did the person get tired? Had someone come along and scared the spiker away? Did the spikes have something to do with Carl Mueller's death?

Eldon's stomach reminded him that it was time for lunch, and that his girlfriend, Sally Rice, worked at the Rockland Burger King where vast quantities of food awaited.

He decided to visit Sally and eat before reporting to Oliver.

Wes whined and stared up at Eldon with sad, longing eyes. The young man looked into Wes' yearning face and wondered how one might smuggle a lively, sixty-pound dog into Oliver's hospital room without attracting attention.

Chapter 16

Sarah had rooted Claude's cell phone out of the clutter in the drawer of his bedside table and found Lurlene's work phone number. Other than a shriek and repeated sobs, Lurlene handled the news that Claude was undergoing emergency surgery reasonably well.

Sarah made the mistake of standing up and beckoning to Lurlene when the girl entered the hospital waiting area. Lurlene pelted across the room, as best she could in her tight skirt, and wrapped her arms around Sarah in a stranglehold that threatened a dislocated neck in addition to strangulation. At least there were no hysterics today, just a low keening sound, punctuated by sobbing noises, and a boa constrictor grip that would have done a professional wrestler proud.

It took a while to gain enough leverage to detach Lurlene's arms, during which time Sarah's pent up rage reached new heights. The day was only half over and here she was, being strangled and slobbered on by the woman who'd stolen her husband.

Free at last, Sarah held her assailant at arm's length and gave her a shake. "Pull yourself together, dammit," Sarah snarled, "before I slap you silly, you little twit!"

"But what are we going to do?" Lurlene wailed.

"The first thing *you* are going to do is stop blubbering, get a grip, and start acting your age," Sarah growled, giving Lurlene another, more vigorous, shake. "You're not helping the situation by getting hysterical. If you really care about Claude, then start being a help instead of a damn pest!"

Sarah glared at Lurlene for a moment and added, "At the very least, sit down over there and shut the hell up!"

Lurlene's doe-like eyes opened wide and she froze as though caught in the headlight of an onrushing train.

Sarah gave the girl a push towards the nearest chair and said, "And fix your face; it's a godawful mess."

Without another word, Lurlene obediently sat and doubled over in as close to a fetal position as one can manage in a waiting room chair. Her body shook gently with silent sobs.

Sarah heaved a sigh, glanced around the room at the nervous faces taking in the scene. "That's right, folks," she thought to herself, "Ogle the crazy lady while she has a meltdown and verbally abuses an innocent child."

Torn between guilt and relief by her outburst, Sarah collapsed beside the heap of misery embodied by Lurlene. "We have to be strong for Claude's sake, Lurlene," she said gently, putting a hand on the girl's shoulder.

There was no response at first, then, faint and muffled, "Is he going to be all right?"

"Of course he is," Sarah replied more firmly than she felt. "Some of the best doctors in the world are working on him right now. They said it would be a few hours before we can see him, but he'll be fine."

Of course that was wishful thinking. Brain injuries, especially after a relapse like this—

"We need to be strong for his sake," Sarah repeated, feeling none too strong herself.

Slowly, Lurlene straightened in her chair and sat, silent and motionless, while she stared across the room with unseeing eyes.

"But what are we going to do?" Lurlene repeated in a small voice.

Sarah looked at her and wondered if the young woman had the slightest inkling of the possible complications. Claude could easily emerge from surgery severely disabled, even vegetative. How would Lurlene handle that? Sarah wasn't sure how she would she handle it, for that matter.

She had assumed that taking care of Claude would be a matter of a few weeks while his broken bones healed, but what if it was worse than that?

"What are we going to do?" Lurlene whined yet again.

"I'm working on it," Sarah replied, thinking that her planning hadn't included the possibility of an injury that might last a lifetime.

Sarah sat for a while in silence. God, she was tired. No, it was beyond tired. It was the exhaustion of being trampled by events beyond her control.

Lurlene sat in silence, contemplating the far wall, unnervingly still.

Sarah got up and left Lurlene after a few minutes and found a quiet spot by one of the waiting area windows. All her phone numbers were gone along with her cell and, irritatingly, Oliver refused to have a cell phone of his own, but it didn't take Sarah long to get the Pen Bay Medical center in Maine.

The phone in Oliver's room rang five times before a woman's breathless voice picked up with, "Hello?"

"Is this Oliver Wendell's room?" Sarah replied, taken aback.

"Yes. He's just coming down the hall. I heard the phone and

came in to get it."

The voice sounded familiar. "Diana?" Sarah said.

"Sarah?" Diana replied. "I thought you were in Boston taking care of your ex-husband."

"I am, but I heard about Oliver's accident and wanted to call—"

"Yes, of course," Diana cut in, sounding flustered. "I heard about it myself on the news yesterday and called him," she paused, then went on in a rush of words. "It sounded as though you'd be away for some time, so I came up to help out for a few days after he gets home."

Diana Carlson, and her husband Frank, had been close friends of Oliver during the years he lived in Boston. Frank had been murdered a few month ago, and Sarah had met Diana at the funeral. She had sensed then that the widow, even in her grief, had her eye on Oliver. In the end, however, Diana had returned to Boston, conceding the field, so to speak, to Sarah. Or so she had thought at the time.

What must Diana have thought on learning that Sarah had gone off to tend to her ex-husband, while Oliver lay in the hospital? God, even Claude had felt that was unreasonable, which was saying a lot.

"How is your ex doing?" Diana asked, breaking into Sarah's thoughts.

"He's in surgery. Again."

"Oh," Diana replied, the single word conveying a whole range of meanings. "Well, here's Oliver now," she added briskly, "trundling in with his IV pole."

"How's Claude doing?" Oliver said. His tone sounded cool when he picked up the phone.

"He's in surgery again. Bleeding in the brain. It will probably be late tonight before they know if there was any permanent damage."

"But the accident was two days ago. What happened?"

"They think there must have been some damage that didn't show up on the CAT scan, and that he got agitated or moved his head wrong, who knows?"

"Im sorry," Oliver replied softly.

"That's not all." Sarah told about her adventures over the last forty-eight hours.

"Jesus," Oliver said when she'd finished. "Do you really think one of the guys who was picketing Ralph's house is connected to this Tony Demano mobster?"

"They certainly look alike."

"Mmm." Oliver sounded skeptical. "Did you get a look at the burglar?"

"No."

"I'm going to have a word with Gaites about his choice of friends," Oliver said grimly.

Sarah decided to change the subject. "Do you know when you can go home?"

"All they'll talk about is drains, like I was some kind of plumbing project gone wrong," he said morosely, "and some infection they keep mumbling about. Apparently, there's a witch's brew of antibiotics in this IV that's supposed to deal with it. Someday."

"At least Diana is keeping you company."

"She arrived yesterday afternoon," he replied, his tone unreadable.

"Staying at the Samoset?" Diana had stayed there before.

"My house. Keeping Wes company."

"I thought she didn't like dogs."

"She doesn't, but she's convinced that I'll be helpless for weeks."

"What do you think?"

"It's not that much worse than when I had my appendix out—no big deal so long as I don't cough, sneeze, or pick up things. I keep telling her that, but she won't listen."

Sarah thought about Diana living in Oliver's house. Would she end up lying in Oliver's bed—the bed she had slept in, albeit just that one time, and then rejected?

"Are you planning to work on *Daisy*?" Sarah said.

"Why not? I'll just go slow."

"The cedar trees had spikes in them?"

"Just one tree so far, but they're still looking."

"The news yesterday talked about spiking trees back in the 1980's, but didn't the tree-spikers tell people about it so nobody would get hurt, like you just did?"

"That was the theory," Oliver said, "but it seems like this tree-spiker forgot about the telling-people part."

"Maybe Carl Mueller spiked the tree and was murdered before he could say anything," Sarah suggested. "Or maybe he got caught doing it and was killed."

"The way he was killed doesn't sound like a spur-of-the-moment kind of thing. Murder-by-tree looks like a statement of some kind, a grudge."

"Spiking trees would be a good way to create a grudge," Sarah said.

"Worked for me," Oliver replied.

"The thing I'm wondering is: what if the tree spiker *did* tell someone?"

"And that person didn't pass on the information?" Oliver paused. "Because it could have held up the timber harvest?"

"If things work out tonight with Claude, I'll go and visit Derwin Denton tomorrow morning," Sarah said.

"For god's sake don't do that. Especially if the mob is mixed up in this. Besides, you've got enough on your mind as it is without taking on the Mafia."

"That's the whole point. I'll go completely out of my mind if I don't get out of here for a few hours." Anything, she thought to herself, that would take her mind off her other problems around Oliver, Claude, and her future.

"So, why don't you just go shopping or—"

"If there's time," she added, ignoring him, "I might be able to drop in on you in the afternoon."

"That's a lot of extra driving—"

"Would you rather I didn't?"

"Of course not," he said irritably. "It's just that you sound exhausted, and you can't have gotten much sleep last night. I don't want you falling asleep at the wheel from trying to drive 400 miles in a day on top of everything else."

"Is Diana in the room?"

"She just stepped out, why?"

"I've been doing a lot of thinking the last two days," she said, "and I'm thinking I'd like to spend the winter in Maine after all. I don't know where I'll stay yet, but I'll be up in a few days, once Claude is settled," she said. If I get him settled, she thought.

"I'm not going anywhere," Oliver replied.

Chapter 17

Later that afternoon, Jack Fournier stuck his head nervously into Oliver's room while Ralph and BB stood in the hallway, looking around as though afraid that some over-zealous nurse might wheel them off to surgery.

"Come on in," Oliver said, from his place in the armchair beside the bed. He had just walked up and down the hall with Diana, and was thinking of getting back in bed to rest. How was it that one could one get so feeble so quickly and better so slowly?

"Just thought we'd see how you was doing," Jack said, as the three men crowded into the room.

Diana, sitting next to Oliver, looked at the new arrivals uncertainly. "Why don't I go down to the gift shop and pick up some magazines," she offered, "so you can have a little more room in here."

"These places make me some nervous," Ralph added after Diana had left. "They ain't healthy, what with all them sick people hanging around."

"As I recollect," BB said to Ralph, "the last time you was in here was when you tore up your leg with a chainsaw. How many stitches was that?"

"Sixty-seven, and I ain't likely to forget that anytime soon, either."

"Me neither," Jack commented. "Never did get all the blood out of the car seat."

The trio looked around the room, shifting their feet uneasily, and smelling of fir and spruce, with an overtone of chainsaw bar oil.

"We been feeling bad about you getting all stove up like this," Ralph said, "where we was the ones who cut them trees."

"It wasn't your fault," Oliver replied. "You had no way of knowing about the spikes. I'd like to get my hands on whoever spiked that tree, though." He nodded at the over-sized nail lying on the bedside table.

Ralph picked it up. "No rust to tell about. Can't have been there long," he commented, passing it to BB.

"They was hoping to get somebody snarled up wicked bad with this," BB added.

"A sixteen or twenty-penny wouldn't have balled things up so bad," Ralph said. "Last time I heard anything like this going on was twenty, twenty-five years ago, up north, around Mount Blue."

"Didn't they send a letter to the paper telling everybody the trees was spiked?" BB said.

"Course they did," Ralph said. "Raised hell and gone with the police tryin' to find out who sent the letter."

Jack returned the spike to the table. "Looks like they just did the cedar trees."

"Damn SOCC," Ralph muttered.

"*Was* it just the cedars?" Oliver said.

"I talked to Bruce Nash this morning," Jack replied, "and that's what he said. 'Course they ain't checked all the trees yet—"

"Take 'em months to do that," BB commented.

"—but there weren't any more around where them cedars was."

"Which tree was it, anyhow," Ralph asked, nodding at the spike.

"The big one," Oliver replied.

"The big, big one?" Jack said incredulously. The three men looked at each other in surprise.

"The biggest log of the bunch, the twenty-footer," Oliver said, looking at his visitors' consternation. "What?"

"That was a standing-dead tree," Jack explained. "The top had broke off probably two, three years ago. That bottom log and a ten-footer above it was all we could save."

"Probably a wind storm did it in," Ralph added. "Cedar can get kinda brittle in the winter."

"Why would anybody spike a dead tree? That's what I don't understand," Jack said.

"Leastways, the police can't put the spiking business on me," Ralph said, "'specially since we was ones cut it down."

Oliver shifted in his chair, yearning for his afternoon nap. "Did they accuse you guys of spiking trees?"

"They asked Ralph about it," Jack said.

"I think they figured Carl Mueller caught me doing it, and I killed him," Ralph said.

"What they ain't figured out is why old Ralph would take that guy way off into the woods just to squash him under a tree," BB said.

"The way *I* figure it," Jack said, "someone else caught Carl Mueller spiking the tree and killed him—"

BB gave a snort. "Like I say, why not just carve him up with Ralph's chainsaw right there on the spot? You know, like that chainsaw massacre movie?"

Ralph had a good four inches on BB, and he glared down at the younger man. "I don't appreciate people talking about killing somebody with my saw. Ain't never going to feel right about using it again."

"You think that saw's got a hex on her now?" BB said sympathetically.

"Wouldn't be surprised if they never give it back, anyhow," Ralph replied sourly.

"Is SOCC still picketing your house?" Oliver asked.

"Not since they went down to picket the cedar trees we cut," Jack said.

"I don't imagine they've got enough people to picket everyone," Ralph said.

———————

Craig Harris shifted his pickup into four-wheel-drive as he swung off the pavement onto the rutted tote road, his headlights carving a tunnel in the darkness. The local sheriff, Bob something-or-other, was, like Craig, doing some off-duty work guarding the Arden Forest Services' motor pool for the night.

The ground was pretty solid here, and Craig figured he'd have no trouble driving his four-by-four right up to the clearing where Arden Forest Services had their machinery parked.

Craig yawned. He'd just gotten off his shift with the Bangor Police Department, and was dead tired. If wasn't that he needed the money—what with his wife expecting any day now—he'd be at home with his feet up and a beer in his hand, instead of spending the night out here in the woods. As it was, the best he could hope for was to catch a few zz's in the truck while he babysat Arden's equipment.

At least machinery didn't complain or give you back-talk all the time—which was what he'd been putting up with most of the afternoon.

He swore as the truck lurched, its headlight beams slashing across the woods as it slipped into a rut he'd missed in the dark. He slowed, shifting into first gear as the vehicle clambered back onto level ground.

He was almost half an hour late in relieving the sheriff, thanks to a three-car pile up on the interstate, and having to crawl through the woods at a snail's pace tried his patience. With a heavy thud, the truck bottomed out on a boulder he'd missed. Craig swore again, slammed into reverse and tried to gun his way back onto solid ground. Instead, the vehicle slid sideways into an even deeper rut.

Craig grabbed his flashlight and got out to survey the scene. To his disgust, he realized that in his rush he'd managed to wander off the tote road in the dark and gotten hopelessly mired on some side track.

Craig figured that he'd either have to get the truck towed out, or risk trashing something expensive trying to get out on his own and end up having to be towed out anyway.

It was cold outside, reminding him that fall was here. He grabbed his flashlight and a backpack containing coffee, supply of junk food, and a radio. Suitably outfitted for the evening, he began trudging down the road. He had a key to the small trailer which served as an office, so at least there was a place to keep warm, but even so, he didn't relish tramping through the woods in the dark.

Craig was so busy watching his footing, muttering about getting stuck, and hoping the sheriff had a truck which could tow him out onto solid ground, that it was a while before he noticed a reddish glow through the trees ahead.

He began to run, slipping on the rutted ground, tripping over roots and rocks, his flashlight beam gyrating across the trees as he struggled to keep from falling.

Somewhere ahead of him an ATV came to life and roared off into the distance.

Craig arrived, panting, at the motor pool and swung his flashlight around the clearing, though he hardly needed the light to see. Not with the timber harvester engulfed in flame. From the look of things, somebody had liberally splashed an accelerant, probably gasoline, on the machine and set it alight. No hope of saving that, he concluded.

The sheriff lay sprawled in the dirt, unconscious. Craig kneeled over the inert form and tried to call for backup on his radio, but he was out of range. He glanced at the sheriff's pickup, saw a short-wave whip mounted above the cab, and breathed a sigh of relief.

The retreating ATV probably meant nobody was around, but Craig kept glancing around as the woods pressed in and the harvester made hissing and popping noises while the flames ate away at the machinery. At least he wouldn't have to worry about staying warm, Craig thought.

The sheriff stirred, moaning.

"It's okay," Craig said. "I'm with the Bangor PD. My name's Craig Harris, by the way. What's yours?" he added as he tucked his coat around the sheriff.

"Bob McAfee. Damn, how long have I been lying here?" He started to get up, and lay down again with a groan. "Guess I'll lie here for a minute."

"Good plan, Hoss," Craig said. "I'll get the EMT's out here to check you out."

"That's going to be a while."

"Not if the radio in your truck can reach outside," Craig said.

"Should work."

"You stay put while I call it in, then," Craig said, as he got to his feet.

He returned a few minutes later, carrying a blanket from Bob's truck. "A bus is on the way," he said, kneeling.

Another ball of flame erupted from the harvester, with a whoomph. Bob flinched at the sound, then groaned and explored the welt on his head gingerly. "Damn, that hurts."

"You see who did it?" Craig asked.

"I heard an ATV off in the woods a little after eight o'clock, but kids run through here all the time, especially on a Friday night like this, so I didn't think much of it. Anyhow, I stepped out of the office trailer and looked around, just to be sure. The next thing I know, you were here."

"Probably parked the ATV somewhere and snuck up on you. I heard one leaving just before I got here."

"Did a good job of waylaying me," Bob said ruefully. He turned his head gingerly to look at the harvester. "Quarter of a million bucks going up in flames over there. Guess Nash won't be sending me a Christmas card this year."

"Hell, he should give you a medal. All the machinery in this clearing would have gone up in smoke if you hadn't been here," Craig replied, thinking that he could have been the one lying on the ground instead of Bob, if he'd gotten here half an hour earlier when he should have. "Besides, Nash must have insurance," he added.

"Still, it seems like a waste," Bob said solemnly, "unless you got some marshmallows in that backpack."

Chapter 18

"Face it, Bruce," Craig Harris said earnestly, "whoever did this probably would have burned everything to the ground if Bob hadn't been here."

"If the damn fool hadn't got himself mugged right out in the open," Bruce retorted viciously, "*nothing* would have gotten burned to the ground." He looked angrily at the smoking ruins of his timber harvester, illuminated by the headlights of half a dozen vehicles.

Other than Bob McAfee, the part-time sheriff, who was now in the hospital for observation, the town of Tyler had no law enforcement, which meant the State Police were investigating the incident—the third time they'd been out here in less than a week, if one counted the tree-spiking investigation.

"Look at it this way," Craig said, trying again, "things could have turned out a lot worse. At least nobody was killed."

"Not yet," Bruce growled darkly, "but if I get my hands on whoever did this—"

"It's just money, and you said the machinery is insured—"

"You think machines like that grow on trees?" Bruce snarled,

oblivious to the irony of his words. "It could take me a week to get
another harvester in here, and I've got a crew coming in first thing
Monday."

"You've still got your skidders and all your other equipment."

Bruce ignored Craig's comment. "SOCC is behind this, and it's
about time someone put an end to them once and for all."

"Let the police handle SOCC, for chrissake."

Craig's feet were getting cold from standing around here so long.
He glanced surreptitiously at his watch and figured it would be well
after midnight before the staties left. No wonder they looked
grumpy—especially the one who was now bearing down on them.

"Whatever you do, don't go making threats in front of the state
cops," Craig hissed. "I know you don't really mean it, but they may
take what you say seriously."

Bruce glared at Craig. "What the hell makes you think I don't
mean it?"

———————

Sarah left Boston promptly at nine o'clock Saturday morning,
heading North.

She had spent the night dozing on a "borrowed" bed at the
hospital—one of the tricks Sarah had picked up during her short
nursing career, before she married Claude.

Sarah felt more rested than she had in days, in spite of her
sketchy sleep, and each mile she put between herself and the
situation in Boston lifted the cloud of gloom, so by the time she hit
the New Hampshire turnpike, the sun, shining down from a
cloudless sky, reflected her mood.

Claude had regained consciousness the previous evening,
confused and having trouble retrieving words. The neurologist had
assured Sarah and Lurlene that Claude would probably make a

"good" recovery—whatever that meant—given enough time. Claude, who considered himself a silver-tongued wordsmith, took the vocabulary glitch with a mixture of anger and frustration.

"Give it a little time, and some therapy," the neurologist had assured him.

"Hell with you," Claude had retorted, demonstrating that some words came more easily to him than others.

For her part, Lurlene had been almost frighteningly subdued since Sarah's outburst in the waiting room yesterday afternoon. Gone were the hysterics, the clinging strangleholds, and best of all, the anguished "Mom" squeals.

Instead, the girl began treating Sarah with deference, if not outright fear. All in all, a big improvement as far as Sarah was concerned, though she felt mildly guilty about the shock she would be inflicting on Lurlene's psyche this afternoon.

Sarah had called Oliver before leaving Boston to tell him she couldn't see him today, but would be up tomorrow for a visit—how long she didn't know yet. He had sounded pleased, perhaps even relieved by the news.

Sarah was so absorbed by her new-found contentment, not to mention her upcoming visit with Derwin Denton, that she didn't notice the maroon Buick, which had been following her from Boston.

———

Derwin Denton was hunched over, head drooping, in a wheelchair which had been parked in a sunny spot by a window in the nursing home's large common area. He was wrapped in a heavy oversized sweater, and looked gaunt and frail.

Sarah pulled up one of the plastic chairs from a nearby table and sat next to him. "Thank you for agreeing to see me," she said.

"I don't get visitors any more," he said, lifting his head to look at her. "My friends are all dead."

Sarah noticed a tremor in his boney hands.

"I wanted to ask you about the woodlot you're having cut up in Tyler," she began.

"So you said when you called this morning," he replied cooly. "That land has been in the Denton family since 1843, and it'll stay in the family as long as I have anything to say about it."

"I wasn't thinking about buying it," Sarah assured the old man, "but I was talking to Jack Fournier, and I happened to see the old cellar hole." She paused, trying to decide how far to spin the truth. The shrewdness in Derwin's eyes as he watched her belied his physical frailty.

"The land is posted, you know," he said, "but if you're a friend of Jack, it's probably all right." He paused. "Better give me a piece of paper, though."

Sarah extracted a notepad and pen from her purse, and handed them to Derwin, who wrote and signed a note giving her permission to go on his land.

"I wrote down the forester's name, Dan Finlon," Derwin said. "He can show you around if you want."

"Thank you," she said, tucking the note into her purse. "I was wondering if you grew up in that house."

Derwin stared across the room, back through time. "I had two brothers and two sisters, all dead now."

"Wasn't that a lot of people for such a small house?"

"Small?" Derwin glanced at her with surprise. "We didn't spend much time in the house during the day, too much work to do, but us boys slept in the loft at night, plenty of space up there, and the girls had a little room off the kitchen—no cellar under that, so it was mighty drafty in the winter."

"I suppose you grew your own food?"

"And then some. It was hard work, but everyone did their share.

Had to. It was that or starve." He looked at her again. "Don't get me wrong. It wasn't all bad. There were a lot of good things, like the peace and quiet, hunting, roaming around in the woods, the smell of lilacs in the spring, eating apples off the tree, vegetables right out of the garden. . ." Derwin caught himself. "But you didn't come all this way to hear an old coot talk about his childhood."

"No," she admitted. "I heard about Ralph and the murder, and was asked to help."

He gazed at her in silence.

"Anyway, I'm curious about Jack Fournier and the cedars he cut."

"What about them?"

"Why not have one person cut the whole lot, instead of splitting the job up?"

Derwin squinted into the midday sun streaming through the window. "Known Jack Fournier all his life. Grew up with his father. Young Jack's a hard worker."

Sarah concluded that Derwin must be well into his nineties. And that he'd avoided answering her question.

"But why have Bruce Nash cut most of the wood?"

Derwin looked at her, irritation flitting across his face. "You'll have to talk to my grandson about that."

"Your grandson?"

Derwin stared out the window again. "My son Dick was a good boy. Loved the farm and the woods, would have stayed on the Home Place if he'd lived."

He turned back to face Sarah again. "Vietnam," he said.

"I'm sorry."

Derwin shrugged slightly. "Kids nowadays don't care about the land, the woods—it's all about money. They think they own the land, but we knew better when we was growing up. Nobody owns the land, not really. We just get a chance to live on it for a while, take care of it as best we know how, and then we're gone."

Sarah sat for a moment, thinking about the old man's surprising eloquence. "So your grandson hired Arden Forest Services?"

"He's a good boy, Young Derwin, goes deer hunting in that woodlot every fall and loves it, but he's no farmer." Derwin sighed. "Young Derwin wants the money quick, says we need it right away, and Jack Fournier can't do the job fast enough."

"But you held out for Jack and the cedars."

Derwin nodded, studying his age-mottled hands as though he hadn't seen them in a long time.

"What about SOCC, the Save Our Cedars Coalition? Have they talked to you or your grandson?"

"Idiots," Derwin replied tersely. "They don't give a damn about the trees. Like everybody else, they just care about money."

He was about to say more, but a tall, husky man, looking to be in his mid-forties, stalked across the room to join them.

"You're the Sarah Cassidy who called this morning," he announced. "I left strict orders that nobody is to visit my grandfather without my prior approval."

"I didn't realize—"

"He's extremely frail, as you can plainly see, and I won't have strangers coming in and upsetting him."

"I wasn't—"

"If you don't leave immediately, I will have you removed from the premises."

"Zip it, Junior," the old man snapped. "It isn't often that a good-looking young lady comes in for a visit, and I'm going to enjoy it as long as I can keep her here."

Sarah glowed with satisfaction, but Young Derwin was not pleased.

"Grandpa, this woman is just trying to sweet-talk you into trouble. The situation is much too complicated for you to be fretting over, so just let me deal with her before you say something you'll regret."

Young Derwin turned to Sarah. "I checked up on you when you called grandpa, and I know your husband is a lawyer and the guy with the sawmill is your boyfriend. If you're here to try and sue us because he got hurt, you're barking up the wrong tree."

Sarah wondered how the man had gotten so much information so quickly. "Did you know that trees had been spiked on your grandfather's land before the accident?" she said.

"Trees were spiked?" the old man exclaimed.

"Let me handle this, grandpa." Young Derwin turned to Sarah. "I'm not going to have you upset my grandfather any more. If you want to talk, we'll do it in private."

They left the old man in his wheel chair, staring out the window into the sunshine, and moved across the room. "Did anybody tell you that trees had been spiked on his land?" Sarah said again.

"An anonymous note," Young Derwin growled, "not that it isn't obvious who did the spiking." He glared at Sarah. "Do you have any idea how much it costs to keep someone in this place? Grandpa needs money from that woodlot *now,* to pay his over-due bills here. They're threatening to toss him out in the street as it is. It's his land and he's got the right to do anything he wants with it."

He shook his head in anger and frustration. "I've been trying to get the damn forester to stop dragging his feet and go over that woodlot ever since spring—had to threaten to fire him before he'd do anything. And now I've got those damn tree-huggers making trouble."

"A man almost died because of those spikes," Sarah snarled. "Doesn't that mean anything to you? Didn't it occur to you that the spikes would be discovered sooner or later?"

"I'm sorry about your friend," Young Derwin said, sounding insincere, "but I have my grandfather's welfare to worry about. God knows how much the mills would knock down the price if they learned some of the trees are spiked."

"Well the cat is out of the bag now," Sarah retorted.

"Mark my words, SOCC will pay for vandalizing those trees," Young Derwin growled.

"You're sure SOCC is behind the spiking?"

"Who else? I go deer hunting in there every November, and I can assure you that there's only the one little stand of cedar in the whole woodlot, but that doesn't stop those people. There's only one way to do that, and it's to hit them in the pocketbook. I'm going to slap them with a lawsuit that'll put them out of business for good."

If you can prove anything, Sarah thought to herself.

Chapter 19

Sarah had driven straight to Muffy's house from Derwin's nursing home, pulling into her friend's driveway by mid-afternoon.

"You want *me* to work with the Realtor and stage your house?" Muffy said incredulously. Surprised as Muffy was—she would never have delegated that sort of job to anybody—Sarah could see an anticipatory gleam lighting up her friend's eyes.

"That's a *huge* responsibility," Muffy added, "but if you're sure you want me to do it. . ." She paused to sip her herbal tea, eyes fixed on Sarah's face.

"Muffy, you know I've always admired your decorating taste." This was an exaggeration, since Sarah's tastes were very different from her neighbor's. On the other hand, Sarah figured that Muffy would have a better idea of what might appeal to the typical Sudbury house-buyer.

Sarah supposed her willingness to hand over the inside if her house to someone else was another sign that she was emotionally letting go of the past, leaving her life in the cellar hole of old memories.

She slid the Realtor's business card across the table. Muffy snatched it up.

"You really aren't coming back, are you?" Muffy said solemnly, taking Sarah's hand. "There's no hope for you and Claude, is there?"

"I have some loose ends to tie up this afternoon, and I'll go up to Maine tomorrow morning for a visit and find a place to stay. I've talked to a Realtor I know up there, and he's going to show me some places to rent."

"So you're not staying with that man, Oliver, you told me about?"

"Don't rush me," Sarah warned. "I need time to be on my own, after Claude."

Sarah arrived at the hospital a little after four o'clock that afternoon and found Claude sitting up in bed with Lurlene in the chair beside him.

Lurlene got up and gave Sarah a sisterly hug before returning to the chair. Claude's eyes widened, shifting his gaze between the two women suspiciously. This was not the behavior he'd come to expect from Lurlene. "W-What's going on?" he said.

Sarah remained standing just inside the door. "Ever since I got here, everybody has been asking me what I was going to do about you after you get out of here, Claude. Well, I've been working on the problem and I have a solution," she announced, turning to the door. "Colleen?"

Colleen entered on cue, while Sarah watched Claude and Lurlene's openmouthed reactions contentedly. "She comes highly recommended and is fully qualified for the position, including experience in working with brain injuries."

From the top of her curly, carrot-red hair to the sensible crepe soles of her shoes, Colleen stood just short of six feet. Her fitted white nurse's uniform revealed a spectacular figure, while her light skin, freckled face, blue eyes, and dimpled smile made her look closer to twenty than her real age of thirty-five.

Colleen smiled engagingly while Sarah recited the woman's many qualifications. Watching Claude's expression while she talked, Sarah began to worry that Colleen might cause another cranial eruption before he'd even hired her.

Lurlene gaped.

Colleen walked over to Claude's bed and shook his hand. "I'm so glad to meet you, Mr. Johnson," she said, the lilt in her voice hinting at her Irish ancestry, and sounding so much like Sarah's long-dead mother that it made her sigh. "I'm sure we'll get along really well. I'm looking forward to working with you."

"Er, yes," he replied, transfixed by the dimples, and unable to release her hand.

Sarah gazed at the scene, wondered if she'd overdone it with Colleen, and quickly rejected the notion as unworthy. The woman was perfect for the job, and qualified people were hard to find.

Colleen extracted her hand from Claude's grasp and stepped over to Lurlene. "I'm glad to meet you too, Miss Phipps," she murmured, taking the girl's limp hand and smiling down at her. "Sarah has told me *so* much about you; I feel like I know you already."

Lurlene mumbled something unintelligible, and gave Sarah a black look.

Sarah, however, was watching Claude with satisfaction. She didn't doubt for an instant that Colleen had the job.

Lurlene, on the other hand, would need to shape up.

"I followed Cassidy up to Denton's nursing home," Vinnie reported.

"I kind of figured she might go there, where she had the phone number," Sal replied. "Doesn't mean anything, 'cause he doesn't know anything."

"The grandson was there too. I saw him go in a little after Cassidy."

Sal wasn't happy about that information.

"Then she went running back to Boston," Vinnie added, "and visited her ex-husband, the lawyer."

"I thought you said he was in the hospital, all banged up," Sal said.

"He is."

"Maybe she was just worried about him, or maybe she's helping her boyfriend sue Denton over those spiked trees."

"Maybe," Vinnie replied, unconvinced, "but you know what Tony says: better safe than sorry. We know she's been nosing around Ralph Barnes and the murder up there."

Sal could understand Vinnie's desire to make an impression on The Thumb, build a rep, but in Sal's opinion the kid was getting too gung-ho over following Cassidy around. Especially where Sal wasn't sure the woman was a threat. Still, he decided, Cassidy would bear watching, especially if she turned up in Maine again.

"What are you driving?" Sal asked.

"The Buick."

"Tony's Buick? Can't you drive your own car for a while?"

"My yellow 'stang?"

"Never mind," Sal replied. The damn Mustang's mufflers could shatter windows a mile away. "How about you rent a car, so she isn't always seeing Tony's Buick in her rear-view?"

"Didn't think of that," Vinnie replied, chastened.

"Keep an eye on her, but not too close. I don't need to know everything she does, what she has for breakfast. And stop breaking into her house, for chrissake."

"Not even for a bug or two?"

"Jesus H. Christ, Vinnie—"

"What about her boyfriend up there? Are you watching him?"

"He's still in the hospital."

"Let me know if you want help up there," Vinnie said, sounding hopeful.

———————

SOCC's narrow storefront headquarters were located in a decaying brick building, sandwiched between an adult bookstore on one side and two trash-filled vacant shops on the other. Behind the building, a rough patch of vacant land fell down to the Kennebec river, where the water was low and sluggish after a dry fall.

It was ten o'clock on Saturday evening, but there was a great stack of mailings, mostly appeals for money, which needed to go out, so Martha Kirkland had stayed late, along with Ken Pourier.

As she stuffed envelopes, Martha marveled at how much money it took to run even a small organization like SOCC. The rent alone on this ratty little place was scandalous.

She remembered wistfully when the whole operation was run from Carl Mueller's kitchen table. It had been like a family then, a close-knit handful of like-minded people working for a caused they believed in passionately. SOCC was bigger now, and she supposed that was a good thing—Ken certainly thought so—but the feeling was different, especially with some of the new people.

The fact was that Martha missed Carl more than she could have imagined possible. She had always admired him for his quirky humor, idealism, and dedication to the cause. She had even allowed herself to daydream about the two of them developing a relationship, but that was gone now. Martha sighed and went back to her envelopes.

Her desk was towards the front, so Martha could serve as a receptionist for the few visitors who dropped in. Behind her was a worktable, and behind that was Ken's desk where he was still at work writing solicitations for money. Monday, he'd start on next month's newsletter, appropriately titled *The Cedar.*

Ken certainly worked as hard as Carl had, but he didn't fill the room with Carl's charm, nor did he tell her as much about his dreams for SOCC.

"You almost done, Martha?" Ken said. He got up and looked at the new posters lying on the work table.

"Just a few more labels, and I can drop the whole batch into a mailbox."

"These placards look really good," he said, picking one up and waving it experimentally. "I like the imagery."

Martha turned in her swivel chair to face Ken and the placard. It showed a cedar tree, standing in a pool of blood, with it's branches drooping in despair. Below it was a chainsaw, dripping blood, behind a circled "X" and the words, "Save Our Cedars." Martha glanced at the thing disgustedly. As far as she was concerned, it was ghoulish and sick, and the bloody chainsaw reminded her of Carl's murder. He would never have used something like that. . .

She lowered her head, fighting back the tears. "Why are we still picketing the Denton lot?" she asked after a moment. "I thought all the cedars were cut."

"It doesn't matter whether they've been cut or not. Denton's woodlot has become a symbol of our cause, and Carl's sacrifice for Maine's forests. Besides, that's where the action is. It's all about publicity, keeping our cause in the public eye."

Martha stared incredulously at Ken. He was beginning to sound more like a politician than an environmental activist.

"Action? You mean vandalism. Arden Forest Services is blaming *us* for torching their equipment, and Denton's lawyer is threatening to sue us over the tree-spiking. What kind of publicity is that?" she demanded.

"It's the kind that's bringing in a lot of new members," Ken said comfortably.

"Lunatics and fanatics, you mean," Martha grumbled. "I wish we could go on to another woodlot." Away from where Carl was murdered, she thought to herself.

"We will, in due time," Ken assured her. "Sal is looking at some possibilities."

"I don't like that man."

"Why on earth not? He's done a lot for SOCC in the last few months."

"I don't think he really cares about the cause, about conservation," she replied. "He seems more—"

A series of explosions filled the room. Shards of flying glass peppered Martha's back as she sat frozen in shock.

She looked up at Ken's face and screamed.

Chapter 20 _____

Sunday morning was warm and sunny, but SOCC's headquarters were dark and gloomy with the front window plywooded over—a gloom that matched Sal's mood. He was not looking forward to the call he would surely receive when Tony The Thumb got the news.

Sal looked at Ken's bandaged face. Slivers of glass had sliced his forehead, cheek, and neck. Sal figured it was lucky the guy wore glasses, or he'd have lost an eye.

"I had no idea this kind of thing would happen," Ken said.

Martha, who was sweeping up bits of glass and plaster dust, gave a snort.

"Think of the publicity," Sal replied encouragingly. "The whole state will know about our cause now."

Martha gave another snort and was rewarded with a glare from Sal.

"When are we going to get a new window?" she demanded. "It's like a cave in here."

"I talked to the landlord about it," Ken replied, "but he wasn't very helpful, said it would take a month."

"*A month?*" Martha exclaimed.

"An organization like this can't have its front window boarded up," Sal announced. "Give me the guy's number and I'll straighten him out."

"I never dreamed this kind of thing would happen," Ken repeated, brooding. "Do you think we've gone too far with our picketing? Did I get our people too worked up?"

"Damn right you did," Martha said tartly.

Ken sighed. "Some of our new members make me nervous. They seem a little too. . . aggressive. Maybe one of them spiked the cedars and burned Arden's machinery. Or even killed Carl."

"Some of our new members are thugs, if you ask me," Martha snapped, wielding her broom viciously.

Ken gazed at the stack of placards. "Maybe we should back off for a while, until things calm down."

"Are you nuts?" Sal retorted. "If we back off now, show any weakness, then the bad guys will have won. We need to stick to our guns. Keep up the pressure. Fight for the cause. Get out and picket the Denton lot. We've lost a day already."

"But who are the bad guys?" Ken moaned. "I'm not sure anymore."

"Did it ever occur to you that *we* have turned into the bad guys?" Martha said as she slammed her broom against the wall and stamped over to her desk. "We've made a hell of a lot of enemies in the last week."

"Bruce Nash already blames us for spiking those cedars and trashing his harvester," Ken pointed out. "And he's just the kind of person who would take a shotgun to our windows."

"You can't make an omelet without breaking some eggs," Sal replied comfortably.

"What the hell does that mean, exactly?" Martha demanded.

"It means we've got a bunch of broken eggs here, so let's take advantage of the situation, build on the free publicity."

"You call this broken eggs?" Martha waved angrily at the plywood.

"Look," Sal said, with exaggerated patience, "it doesn't matter who did what, it's the principle of the thing. We have to stand up for what's right even if we make some enemies."

"Enemies who shoot up our window? If he had aimed lower, we'd be dead, you idiot!" Martha screeched.

Ken sat at his desk, cradling his bandaged face.

———

Eldon thought that Sally Rice looked really good in her phony uniform with the words "Therapy Dog Handler" stenciled across the front. But then Eldon thought his girlfriend looked good no matter what she wore. Or didn't wear.

Wes enjoyed his new role as he dragged Sally down the hospital corridor. The dog's brain was nearly bursting with new aromas, as well as the scent of his master, who had been shuffling up and down this very hallway not long ago.

"Weston Farmer, heel," Sally said firmly, as she tugged at the leash.

Wes looked at her disgustedly and stationed himself beside her, willfully bumping into her right leg.

"I still think the laundry hamper idea was better," Sally commented, lurching a bit under Wes' onslaught.

"He would never have stayed still long enough in there," Eldon replied.

Sally staggered as Wes gave her a particularly strong nudge.

"Heel," Sally repeated with another tug. "What was wrong with the Gurney idea, then? Sure there were problems with it, but we could have strapped him down—"

"Where are you going with that animal?" They looked up to see an officious figure marching down the hall towards them.

"Here comes trouble," Eldon muttered.

"I'll handle this," Sally replied.

"Therapy dog," Sally told the nurse, "to visit room—"

"214," Eldon prompted.

"You're not taking that dog anywhere without checking in," the nurse said as she escorted them to the nurses' station.

———

Sarah had arrived a few minutes before Sally, Eldon, and Wes, so she missed seeing them being marched away—which was probably for the best.

She knocked tentatively at the open door, unsure what to expect.

What she found was Oliver in his bed, tray table in front of him, eating lunch. Alone.

Sarah leaned over and kissed his cheek. He was running a fever.

He turned his head and kissed her on the lips. "That's better," he said after a moment.

Sarah cast a professional eye on th IV pole. "How do you feel?"

"Spacey. They're trying a new cocktail this morning," he said, catching her glance. "Might be working."

Sarah scanned the room. "Where's Diana?"

"I sent her home."

"You sent her home? Just like that? After she came all the way up here? I hope she wasn't too upset."

"Upset?" he said, clueless for a moment. "It was kind of mutual, really. She told me she figured she'd better leave as soon as you called the other day."

Sarah perched gingerly on the edge of the bed. "I'm sorry about walking out on you like that, without really talking about things, but Claude's accident derailed me."

Oliver gazed across the room. "How is Claude?" he said.

"It's not like that," she said, answering his implied question. "But he's better, and I've got him settled."

"Settled? That sounds ominous. For him. Good in another way, but ominous."

"He and I are ancient history."

"Like an old cellar hole?"

Sarah looked at him, thinking that the man had a knack for disconcerting her. "Maybe it was the accident—the head injury—but he's different. Ever since the divorce he's been chasing me around like a lovesick octopus, trying to get me back, but yesterday, when he heard you were in the hospital, he bawled me out for not being up here."

Oliver looked at her, a trying to suppress a smile. "A lovesick octopus? This hasn't been a good summer for you, has it?"

"In a lot of ways, no." She took his hand. "In other ways, yes."

"Good answer."

"The thing is," she said, still holding his hand, "I need space. It's only been seven months since the divorce. I need time."

"I understand."

She looked at him, thinking it had been some ten years since his wife had died. "I know you do," she said.

"I didn't mean to pressure you about moving in with me. It was just a suggestion, because it didn't sound as if you had anywhere to stay over the winter."

"I talked to Brian on the phone yesterday about renting a place."

Brian Curtis, Burnt Cove's Realtor, had shown a romantic interest in Sarah over the summer. Another complication in her life. "He's going to show me some possibilities tomorrow."

Oliver knew about Brian's interest. "Mmm," he said. "Where will you stay until you find a place, a motel?"

"I'll stay with you for a while. You're going to need some help around the house, after all."

"No offense," Oliver said, staring at her, "but women are a total mystery to me. Especially right now."

"That's as it should be," she replied, kissing him again.

"How much of a fever are you running?" she said after a while.

"Now, or before you came in?"

"Seriously."

"Can't remember. A hundred and something?"

They heard a sudden scrabbling noise, followed by Wes, who was strangling himself against his collar as he fought for traction.

"Wes, you furry fraud," Oliver said as Sally was dragged into the room. "What kind of scam have these con artists gotten you into now?"

"Hey, give the dog a break. He's been a wreck ever since you disappeared," Eldon said.

"Don't jump on my stomach!" Oliver yelped as Wes jerked his leash out of Sally's grasp, and launched himself across the room and onto the bed.

Some canine instinct made the warning unnecessary. Wes tiptoed into a position where he could lick his master's face. With a satisfied whine, he lay down, his head on Oliver's chest, his nose tucked under Oliver's chin.

"They don't call them Springer Spaniels for nothing," Eldon commented.

Sarah took in the scene, struggling for composure. She'd known these people—correction: these people and this dog—for a summer, and already they'd won her heart.

Wes, sensing his master was the wrong temperature, began licking Oliver's face.

"Gimme a break, dog," Oliver pleaded, suppressing a grin.

"We can't stay long," Sally said. "Wes has a list of visits to make."

"Visits?" Sarah said.

"Sure. He's a Therapy Dog," Eldon replied.

"You can't be serious about this therapy dog scheme," Oliver said worriedly. "He doesn't have any training."

"He loves to have his ears scratched, wags his tail a lot, and pants like mad," Eldon pointed out. "What more does he need?"

"What about the jumping on beds thing? What about all the licking?"

"We'll have to keep an eye on that," Sally conceded, "but he's a quick learner."

Chapter 21

"I have a bad feeling about this therapy dog business," Oliver said as Sally dragged a reluctant Wes out of the room for his round of visitations.

"He'll have a ball," Eldon reassured him. "Besides, Sally's right there, so what could possibly go wrong?"

"Didn't Maxwell Smart say that on TV just before the roof fell in?" Oliver replied.

"How long is he going to be doing his rounds?" Sarah said.

Eldon shrugged. "Don't know. Half an hour, maybe? Sally's the expert."

Oliver rolled his eyes.

"I can take Wes back to the house with me when he's done, if his visiting doesn't take too long," Sarah said, "but I'm meeting Brian Curtis at two o'clock."

"There's no need to go out of your way," Eldon replied. "We can drop him off."

"I'm going over anyway to unpack my bags, so it's no problem. I'll need a key, though."

"Okay," Eldon said, keeping his voice carefully neutral. "You can use Sally's key, then. She won't need it if you're there."

"Diana's key is in the bedside table drawer," Oliver said. "You can have that one."

"Diana had a key?" Sarah said.

"Everybody on the East Coast has a key to my house," Oliver muttered.

Except for me, Sarah thought. She decided to change the subject. "How is Ralph doing?"

"Not good," Eldon replied. "The cops have him up a tree again over the harvester."

"Why do they think he had anything to do with that?" Sarah said.

"Probably because they think he killed Carl Mueller with his chainsaw," Eldon said. "They must figure there's some kind of connection."

"Some kind of grudge thing involving Ralph?" Sarah suggested.

"Maybe it is," Oliver said. "The trouble is, everybody has a grudge against everybody else by now. SOCC blames Ralph for killing Carl Mueller, Bruce Nash blames SOCC for torching his equipment, SOCC blames Bruce for shooting up their headquarters, Ralph blames Bruce and SOCC for framing him, everybody blames SOCC for the tree spiking, and Briskin is driving SOCC crazy by derailing their protests. And speaking of grudges, you can add my name to the list."

"SOCC was shot up?" Sarah exclaimed.

"Last night," Oliver replied. "Someone fired three rounds from a shotgun into the building. Blew in the whole plate glass window. Ken Pourier got his face cut up. The police think somebody parked across the street and waited until the coast was clear before blasting away."

"Ken was on the early morning news," Eldon added, "all

bandaged up and swearing that SOCC will keep on picketing Denton's woodlot."

"It turns out, by the way," Sarah said, "that Young Derwin Denton had been told about the tree spiking but didn't say anything for fear the mills wouldn't pay as much for his grandfather's logs."

"That was thoughtful of him," Oliver grumbled.

"I'm going up tomorrow and have a look around," Sarah said casually.

Oliver lurched upright, stifled a groan, exclaimed, "Are you crazy!"

"I knew you wouldn't like it—"

"I hate it! You're nuts!"

"—but I'm doing it anyway. Something up there got Carl Mueller killed—"

"And you're going to find something the cops missed? Without getting killed yourself?"

"A fresh pair of eyes can't hurt," Sarah replied stubbornly, "and I'll be perfectly safe."

"You shouldn't go up there all alone," Eldon said. "I'd go with you, but Pearly is up to his ears hauling boats and I need to help him."

"For god's sake, you two," Sarah retorted, "I have no intention of going by myself. I'd probably get lost wandering around there anyway, so I called Dan Finlon, the forester who is working for Derwin on the woodlot. Derwin gave me his name, and he seemed nice when I talked to him on the phone, and he'll be up there anyway. I'll meet him tomorrow morning."

Oliver nodded, mollified. "He was in here a couple of days ago. Seemed okay. Doesn't care much for SOCC."

"He can't be all bad, then," Sarah said.

A sudden crash, followed by a scream and a shouted, "Weston!" erupted in the hallway.

The sound of claws scrabbling for traction on the floor heralded Wes, who bounded into the room and leaped onto Oliver's bed.

Sally followed, swearing under her breath. "Little monster yanked the leash right out of my hand. Again."

Wes flattened himself out alongside Oliver, and he peered defiantly at Sally from his refuge behind Oliver's chest.

Just then, the head nurse stalked through the door. Wes pancaked himself even lower behind Oliver, wagging his tail tentatively as he looked at the imposing figure.

"I'm sorry about the food cart," Sally said. "I'll take Wes away."

The head nurse shook her head, suppressing a smile as she looked at Wes' imploring face. "I suppose he can stay a little bit longer while they're cleaning up the mess. Just keep the door closed."

Wes, sensing a reprieve, lifted his head and panted happily at her.

"Don't expect a therapy dog medal from me," the nurse told him.

———

"How is the weather up there?" Tony inquired.

Sal made a conscious effort to loosen his grip on the phone. He figured that Tony's question could mean several things. That was the trouble with being someone like The Thumb—you always had to assume your phone was tapped.

"Been pretty warm all week," Sal replied, meaning the words figuratively. "Still got tourists coming up," he added, referring to Sarah's arrival. "But we should get a frost in a week or so."

"You should take care of yourself, Salvatore. I worry about you working too hard."

The Thumb was obviously worried that things were headed for hell. "I'm fine, Uncle Tony. In fact, I'm taking a walk in the woods with some friends tomorrow."

Tony understood that Sal was referring to SOCC. "That's good, Sal. I hope you have a good time." There was a pause. "You going with your friend, Ken?"

"Yeah. I don't dare let him go off by himself. The guy gets lost in the woods so easy."

"You better keep a good eye on him, then. It's not good for somebody to lost in the woods up there."

"Especially this time of year," Sal agreed. "It can get real cold at night."

"Don't get lost yourself, Salvatore," Tony said with a laugh that wasn't quite a laugh.

"I got a GPS, Uncle Tony, so I'm all set," Sal said. "And I'll be back in a few weeks." Sal fervently hope that was true. He longed for the city, the bustle, the people, his friends. The longer he stayed here the more homesick he got.

"I hear Vinnie is up there for a visit," Tony commented.

"He came up this morning, Uncle Tony. I talked to him on the phone." Sal didn't need to explain that Vinnie was here because that pesky Cassidy woman had turned up in Maine again. He still wasn't convinced that she was a threat, but if Tony, who had an instinct for these things, was worried, then Sal figured he'd better worry too. "Me and Vinnie are going to get together this afternoon," he said.

"You two seem to get along pretty good."

Sal knew that was really a question. "Yeah, its great having him around."

"Vinnie's a good kid, plenty of enthusiasm," Tony said.

Sal didn't mind the enthusiasm part except when Vinnie went off and did something stupid, like breaking into Cassidy's house.

Sal thought about the Denton woodlot business, where things looked to be getting out of control. It was strange the way you could give something a little nudge and find out you were pushing on a house of cards when you thought it was a brick outhouse. "There are some things Vinnie can help me with if he's going to be around for a while."

"I'm sure he'd love to help out," Tony assured him.

Sal figured Tony was giving him a blank check with Vinnie, not to mention a vote of confidence.

"We should get together for lunch next week," Tony added. "Give me a call when you got some time free."

Okay, so maybe the blank check had strings attached.

———

Sarah turned into Oliver's rutted dirt driveway, which ran uphill a hundred yards across a field to the house. Wes stood on the seat beside her, wagging and whining excitedly. Dogs had such simple needs, she mused. Someone to love and care for them, a place to call home, and they were content. How easy compared to the complexities of human entanglements. She glanced at Wes. On the other hand, perhaps he had something to teach human beings about relationships.

Wes turned and panted joyfully at her as she patted his back.

Sarah let herself into Oliver's house through the kitchen door and stood, taking in the scene. Diana had wasted no time in leaving her mark on the place. Oliver's normal kitchen clutter was gone, replaced by an antiseptic cleanliness, laced with the aroma of soap and air freshener. The floor glistened, while the counters were stripped bare of the usual assortment of stray dishes, carelessly scattered cooking utensils, half-eaten loaves of bread, and other odds and ends. She figured it would take Oliver a month to find where everything was stored.

Wes sidled by her and drank thirstily from his water bowl, splashing the area liberally in the process.

Sarah wandered, bemused, through the house. Diana must have spent every spare minute cleaning and tidying. How long had she been here?

There was no way to tell whether Diana had slept in Oliver's room or the guest bedroom, though a vase of cut flowers adorned the bureau in Oliver's room. Sarah scolded herself for wondering about such things. She was aware that Diana and Oliver had known each other well, perhaps intimately, before they'd married others. Was it unreasonable for one, or both, of them to dream of rekindling the old flame?

Besides, she reminded herself, nature abhors a vacuum. She had gone down to Boston; Diana had come up to Maine. It was simple symmetry.

Still, Diana had managed to put a lot of herself into the house in a very short time.

Immersed in thought, Sarah carried her bags upstairs, placing them in the spare bedroom.

She had just returned to the kitchen and fed Wes when her cell chimed.

"You are a vicious, heartless, sadistic woman!" the voice screamed in her ear.

"Lurlene," Sarah replied brightly. "How nice to hear from you. I was just going to call and see how you all were doing."

"You have got to make that witch go away," Lurlene said, her voice dripping with fury.

"Witch? Do you mean Colleen?" Sarah replied, thinking that rage could be an improvement over Lurlene's usual child-like helplessness.

"Who else would I mean!"

"But Lurlene, dear, that's up to Claude, not me. After all, he hired Colleen, so he's the only one who can fire her," Sarah said reasonably. "Why don't you talk to him about your concerns?"

"The witch has moved into his apartment!" Lurlene snarled.

"But that's good, isn't it? That must mean Claude is coming home from the hospital soon, doesn't it? And it must mean that he won't have to spend weeks in rehab, doesn't it? And he'll certainly need somebody with him 24/7 for at least a few days, won't he?"

"You hired her for her looks, because she's so young," Lurlene said shrewdly. "You did it just to get back at me, you vicious, nasty, vengeful. . ." Lurlene sputtered out, words failing her.

"Colleen is thirty-five years old," Sarah said calmly. "She just happens to be one of those lucky women who look ten or fifteen years younger than their real age—"

"He practically drools when he looks at her!"

"Of course he does. I was married to him, remember? The thing is, nobody can stay young forever, not Colleen, not you, not me, and not even Claude—"

Lurlene wailed into the phone.

"Listen to me, you little twit," Sarah said forcefully. "If you want to keep Claude, you're going to have to make him care about *you* and not just your looks. Help him with his therapy. Tidy up his apartment. Get him a potted plant, or a pair of slippers. Be more than just eye-candy, for heaven's sake."

Even as she spoke, Sarah wondered who she was preaching to.

After all, that advice hadn't saved her marriage to Claude.

Chapter 22

The Monday morning air was cool and crisp as Sarah pulled her Ford Explorer in behind a row of cars parked at the pavement's edge. A thin row of scrubby trees lined the road, and behind them she could glimpse a clearing with a pile of freshly cut logs in it. The roar and whine of machinery, accompanied by the scream of chain saws told her that Bruce Nash and his crew were working somewhere on the far side of Denton's woodlot.

She climbed out of the Explorer and took in the scene, barely recognizing the place for all the changes that had taken place in the last week: a clearing beside the road hacked out of a stand of young trees, the muddy, rutted tote road they had explored earlier covered over with fresh gravel, and most of all, a crowd of picketers waving signs and clogging the tote road. Sarah started to approach them uncertainly.

"Sarah Cassidy?"

She saw a tall, husky, forty-ish man approaching.

"Dan Finlon?" she replied.

"That's me," he said, shaking her hand with a firm grip. Closeup, in a heavy chamois shirt, jeans, and boots, he looked to be a man who spent a lot of time outdoors.

"I'm glad you have a written note from old man Denton," Dan said. "Bruce Nash won't be too happy to find me showing you around, but I work for Derwin, so to hell with Bruce."

"Bruce didn't seem like a friendly sort when we bumped into him the other day," Sarah commented.

"He's having his share of problems," Dan replied. "There's a pulp truck on the way," he added, "and I think we'd better ride in that instead of walking."

"I don't mind walking."

"I'm sure you don't, but that bunch of picketers is blocking the access road, and I'd just as soon not have to push my way through them."

Sarah was close enough now to see the group—nine or ten people—blocking the track, waving signs and chanting.

"SOCC?" she said. "Do you think they'd try to stop us?"

"Damn lunatics. God knows what they might try, but I don't want to take any chances. The cops have been called, but it may be a while before they get here to clear them out of the way."

Soon, they heard a pulp truck lumbering up the road. With a hiss of air brakes, it eased over to the side of the pavement and stopped beside them. Sarah instantly recognized the bushy eyebrows gazing down at them from the cab.

"Pastor Briskin," she said.

"Sister Sarah, what a blessing to see you again," he replied.

"You two know each other?" Dan said, surprised.

"We met a couple of months ago," Sarah replied, impressed that Briskin remembered her name from their brief encounter.

"How is brother Oliver?" Pastor Briskin said as he leaned out the open window, his wildly unkempt hair blowing in the breeze. "I heard about his accident, and we said a prayer for him Sunday."

"He was a lot better this morning when I called. His fever is down, and they think he'll be able to go home this afternoon. I'll stop in and see him on my way home."

"Great is the power of the Lord!"

Dan gave a snort. "More likely the power of antibiotics."

The bushy cleric beamed at Dan with the contented expression of a good-natured bear who has just discovered a honeycomb. "And who do you think gave us antibiotics?" he inquired. "The Lord, who gives us all things," he added, answering his own question.

"Preach to someone else if you want, but we're just looking for a lift," Dan said.

"Climb aboard, then," Pastor Briskin replied. He looked at the picketers while Sarah and Dan clambered into the truck. The activists were clearly energized by sight of such a juicy target.

"Let us pray," Pastor Briskin said thoughtfully as his passengers seated themselves, "for those misguided souls as they are scattered beneath the wheels of righteousness."

"Jesus, let's not run over anybody," Dan said, nervously eying Briskin—an imposing figure in a worn hoodie and blue-jeans. And a grim expression.

"I shall pray that they repent of their heathen tree worship and come to Jesus before Satan gathers them in to eternal hell-fire."

"Just don't get carried away," Dan pleaded.

"I have met these people before," Pastor Briskin murmured enigmatically as the truck crept forward.

The picketers were working themselves into a frenzy of shouted slogans as the truck approached.

None of them seemed ready to step out of the road.

"Maybe we should walk after all," Dan suggested.

"We are here to do God's work," Pastor Briskin informed him as the truck crawled forward at a slow, inexorable walking pace.

They were within ten feet now and nobody was giving ground.

"Whatever that work may be," Briskin added grimly.

Sarah looked at the crowd and saw the Tony Demano look-alike who had been picketing Ralph Barne's house. He stared back at her with a frown. He was standing a little apart from the rest of the picketers, with a tall, skinny younger man at his side. Was it her imagination, or did the two bear a family resemblance?

Pastor Briskin leaned out the open truck window. "Where is your bible in this time of trial, my brother?" he bellowed.

Ken looked up at the truck, dismay etched on his face.

The truck was inching forward at a crawl now, its engine roaring, only a few feet between it and the picketers.

The truck's air horn let out an ear-splitting blast.

"For God's sake stop!" Dan yelled.

His warning was unnecessary for the SOCC group, recognizing Briskin, scattered.

"You could have killed those people," Dan said as they rumbled by.

"There was no danger, brother Dan, once they recognized me," Pastor Briskin replied placidly. "They must have taken comfort in knowing that I was praying for their misguided souls."

"That guy is crazy, a damn religious fanatic," Dan Finlon said as the holy pulp truck rumbled by them on its way up the tote road to pick up its load of wood. Dan looked back, where the picketers had returned to their posts across the road about a hundred yards behind them. The group were shouting, waving signs, and milling about like a hive of uprooted bees.

"I drove a pulp truck for a while after college," Dan went on, "and they can't stop all that fast, even when they're empty. He could have killed one of those people, not that I've got any use for that bunch."

Sarah doubted that Pastor Briskin would have actually run over anybody, though, looking back on it, she wasn't absolutely sure. Would he have stopped, or been able to stop, if one of the picketers had slipped and fallen beneath the "wheels of righteousness?" Several of the signs had met just that fate, dropped in the frantic rush to escape.

Dan wore a blaze-yellow vest with spacious pockets, from which he removed a hand-drawn map. "Let's orient the map," he said, facing down the tote road with his back to the picketers. "We're here, facing East" he added, pointing to a spot on the map. "Up ahead on the left is the clearing where Bruce's timber harvester got torched. He's enlarged the clearing and brought in a lot of gravel, so he can use the space to yard out timber, once the police let him start cutting on this part of the lot."

"We got that far last week before Bruce chased us away."

"He's managed to lease another machine," Dan added, "got two people guarding it now. I'm told they have orders to shoot first, so I wouldn't come in here after dark."

Dan turned to the map. "The lot is rectangular, about a mile wide on the paved road, and almost two miles deep. As you can see from the map, the access road comes in from the tarred road at about the middle of the lot. Bruce has extended the access road beyond the clearing, so it now turns left and runs up to the northern side of the lot. That's where they're cutting now. We can walk up there and see what they're doing if you like. I haven't been down to the southeast corner yet, but Bruce will put in an access road down there when I've gotten to it."

"The southeast corner?"

"It's up about a mile or so ahead on the right."

Dan paused and looked at Sarah. "It would help if I knew what you were looking for, so we don't waste the morning just walking around at random."

"I'm not really sure what I'm looking for, except that I'd like to see where Jack Fournier took out the cedars."

"That's easy, it's about a half mile beyond Bruce's machinery depot, on the left."

"Do you know the spot where Carl Mueller was killed?"

"Yes."

"I'd like to see that too."

"Fine. It's just beyond the cedars on the right," he said, pointing in a vaguely two o'clock direction. "It's pretty rough going, and there's not much to see. They had to cut up the tree to get it off him, and the ground is all chewed up with tire tracks."

"Still—" she replied.

Dan shrugged. "Fine. Derwin said to show you around, so I'll show you around. Let's start with the cedars, since they're the closest."

He set off at a brisk pace.

The road led through a stand of huge pine trees. Sarah paused, looking at them in awe.

Dan rested his hand gently, almost reverently, on one of the tree trunks. "All these trees look good, but they've pretty much reached their full potential. Time for them to be thinned out and make room for new growth," Dan commented, his voice tinged with regret.

"The cycle of life and death?"

"I guess that makes Bruce Nash the Grim Reaper," Dan said with a thin smile, "though Bruce will have to wait on these trees until the police are done with their investigations."

"A reprieve," Sarah commented.

Dan paused, seeming to give himself a mental shake. "Actually, when people use the term 'tree farming,' they mean it literally. What we're doing here is harvesting a crop. You wouldn't leave a stand of grain out in the field once it was ripe. It would be a waste, and leave a mess when it was time to plant in the spring."

"Yes, but trees live a lot longer than grain," Sarah pointed out. "Besides, harvesting a crop of grain doesn't leave as big a mess behind."

Dan gave her an intent look. "Trees are magnificent things, living hundreds even thousands of years, yet a lot of people think nothing of cutting them down without a second thought. That's why there are timber harvesting laws, and that's why I became a forester, to protect the forest." Dan paused. "We'll actually take less than half of the trees in here. It's all about moderation, after all, harvesting a resource while doing as little damage as possible."

They walked on and the big pines soon gave way to younger trees, a mixture of hardwood and softwood.

Dan stopped. "Listen," he said. "Hear the birds and the squirrels? This area was selectively cut over maybe twenty years ago."

Standing quietly, Sarah could hear the faint sounds and rustles of small animals, almost drowned out by the whine and roar of Bruce's heavy machinery.

"The young saplings and brush provide food and shelter for deer and small animals," Dan went on. "The woods here are alive and growing. Those big pines may look nice, but they've shaded out all the young growth so there's no place for animals. There's no life there. The big pines have taken it all for themselves." He turned to Sarah, the intensity of his gaze making her uneasy. "That's something those SOCC people don't understand—the basic principle of life—that some things have to die for others to live. Even their precious cedars."

The cedar stumps, when they got there, didn't reveal any secrets, as far as Sarah could see.

"I marked the bigger trees, so they wouldn't take them all," Dan said, "and had Fournier thin some of the junk wood to release the smaller cedars—"

"Release?"

"Open up around them so they'll get more sun and space to grow, and less competition."

Sarah looked around and saw perhaps a dozen young cedar trees scattered through the freshly cut clearing.

Dan put his foot on one of the stumps. "Here's the standing dead tree with the spikes in it."

"Just the one cedar tree was spiked?"

"Yes. Strange to spike just one tree, but it sure stirred up a lot of trouble."

Chapter 23

A short way beyond the cedars, they came on a line of ATV tracks crossing the tote road. "Is that where Carl was killed?" she said, thinking the police might have made the tracks.

Dan shook his head. "Kids," he replied sourly. "They've got trails all through here—rutting up the woods, breaking down sap-lings—drives young Denton crazy. He's got the land posted and he's complained to the sheriff a hundred times, but there's no way to stop the ATVs, not with all the empty land out here."

Dan strode on. "The spot is right up ahead," he said over his shoulder.

They soon came to a place where the tote road bore off to the left, while a beaten down a track lead off to the right. They followed the track, saplings and thick brush pressing in on both sides. After a few minutes the track ended in a clearing.

"A natural clearing," Dan commented. "It's all ledge here, not enough soil for trees, except for the one beech that somebody dropped on Mueller."

"Where are we on the map?"

Dan pulled the map out of his pocket, unfolded it, and pointed to a spot.

"We're pretty close to the south side of Derwin's land," Sarah commented.

"And about three-quarters of a mile from the paved road," Dan said. "The ledge we're standing on drops off into a big marshy area that runs up to the far corner on his lot," Dan added, pointing. "I haven't gone in there yet, because the ground is too soft to get machinery into the area until we have a hard freeze."

Sarah could see what Dan meant. There was an abrupt drop-off of nearly twenty feet, just beyond the fallen beach tree.

"There are a lot of trees down there, even if it is marshy," Sarah said.

"We'll get to them in due time, but a lot of those big hemlocks will probably be rotten in the center; they don't like having their feet wet."

"The police certainly went over the area, looking for clues," Sarah went on, staring at the flattened ground.

"All they found was Ralph's chainsaw, as far as I know."

"Was there a path into here before the police opened it up?"

"Not to this spot," Dan replied.

"And the tote road wasn't here when Carl was killed?"

"Not until they put it in the other day. There was just the ATV trail we crossed a little way back."

"It must have been hard work to push through all that brush, carrying a chainsaw, especially for an old man like Ralph," Sarah commented.

Dan smiled at her. "Don't kid yourself. That old man is tough as shoe leather. After all, he's been carrying chainsaws through the woods all his life. Besides, he could have had an ATV, and come in on their trails."

Sarah gave herself a mental kick for not having thought of that possibility. It was one thing to carry a chainsaw a mile or more through the woods, quite another to drive an ATV. "Does the ATV trail go over to where Ralph is working?"

Dan shrugged. "Don't know for sure, but I wouldn't be surprised."

"I wish I knew why anybody would come all the way out here to kill someone with a tree."

"If you knew why," Dan said with another shrug, "you'd probably know who."

———

While Sarah and Dan were looking over the crime scene, Pastor Briskin was easing his heavily laden truck along the tote road. The pulp wood he was carrying had been checked by Bruce's metal detector and was destined for the paper mill in Bucksport, which happened to be offering a good price this week.

Briskin was relieved to see the SOCC picketers were no longer blocking the road. In fact, two state police troopers had pushed them back across to the far side of the pavement, leaving plenty of room for his truck to swing onto the main road. He gave a short toot of his air horn as he pulled out, waving at the picketers as he passed.

He was greeted with a chorus of yells and catcalls for his trouble, though one of the smokies gave him a grin and a thumbs-up. The cleric/trucker resolved to pray for SOCC's enlightenment later, but it was eleven o'clock and his stomach was rumbling—a situation that was not conducive to prayers for SOCC, or anybody else.

Pastor Briskin knew that his wife had put a couple of sandwiches and an apple in his lunch bag. He'd already drunk from the oversized thermos of coffee.

It was hilly country here and the constant need to work through the gears made eating impractical for the moment, stomach rumbles notwithstanding. He would find a place to pull over and eat when he got to Monroe. From there on, it was good roads all the way to Bucksport.

The truck clambered slowly up a hill, and Briskin worked his way up through the gears as he hit the level.

He approached the next downslope at a good rate of speed, hoping to slingshot himself at least part way up the next hill.

About half way down the slope, however, an elderly gent in a battered pickup suddenly pulled out of a dirt road onto the pavement.

"Bless you, my brother," Pastor Briskin muttered as he hit the brakes. There would be no sling-shotting up the next slope now, Briskin thought to himself. He'd have to laboriously crawl all the way at a snail's pace.

The brake pedal suddenly went to the floor and Briskin caught a glimpse of a warning light out of the corner of his eye.

He was now closing on the pickup like an avenging angel—an angel with no brakes.

Briskin hit the horn, knowing it was far too late to do any good. The top-heavy pulp truck swerved, teetered, jack-knifed, and slid on its side into the trees.

———

Sarah had left Dan Finlon so the forester could go and check on Bruce's wood cutting while she walked back out to the paved road.

She was glad to find the state police had moved SOCC's picketers out of the way. Retrieving her Explorer, she drove the mile or so to where Jack and his crew were working, the spot marked by Jack's aged Chevy Nova and Ralph's equally aged pickup. Sarah glanced into Ralph's truck as she walked by. The back was filled with cans of oil, spare tires, lengths of chain, and various odds and ends, but no chain saw.

Nash was cutting on the side of Denton's woodlot adjacent to this one, and the noise of his machinery sounded close by as she hiked into the woods to find Jack's crew. Her muscles were beginning to complain about the unaccustomed exercise, and she was getting tired of tramping down rutted tote roads. After a while, though, she came to the three men.

"Well look who's here," Jack Fournier said as Sarah walked into the clearing where Jack's crew were eating their lunch.

"You walk in from the road to have lunch with us?" BB said. "We figured you must have given up on poor Ralph, where we ain't seen you for a while."

"I had to go down to Boston for a few days."

The men nodded silently and ate some more of their sandwiches.

"We'll try and get a couple more twitches out this afternoon," Jack said to BB after a moment, "finish up that load."

"Keep old Ralph working," BB replied.

Ralph took a swallow of coffee from his thermos.

They were ignoring her now, either in disapproval of her going away and neglecting Ralph and his problems, or simply waiting for Sarah to say why she was here.

"I was just looking at the place where Carl Mueller was killed," she said, "and I've got some questions."

They looked at her in silence.

"Do you know if there's an ATV trail running from this area up to where Carl was killed?" she said.

"So now you think Ralph hopped onto an ATV and went up to kill Mueller?" Jack said cooly.

Sarah realized that she wasn't handling this well. The combination of fatigue and nervousness was doing her in. "No I don't, but I was wondering if you had heard an ATV going by about the time he was killed. It would be another way the killer might have gotten in there."

The three men looked at each other, tension in the air almost palpable.

"There's ATV trails all over this country, goin' every which way," BB said after a while.

"We hear them in the woods all the time," Jack said. "Don't pay them any attention."

"Wouldn't have heard them anyhow, if we had a saw running," BB added.

Ralph took another bite of his sandwich.

"I can't say we heard an ATV that morning," Jack concluded. "Then I can't say we didn't."

"Guess maybe I don't need you helping me with the police any more," Ralph murmured.

"What? Why not?"

"They ain't been around for a couple of days—"

"Not since they came and asked about how Nash got his machinery burnt up," BB interjected.

"—so I figure they've gone off on somebody else and you and your friend can leave it be," Ralph said.

———

Brian Curtis, Burnt Cove's resident Realtor, was in his mid-fifties, with thinning blonde hair, a winningly boyish smile, and an easy manner.

"What a nice surprise," he said, flashing Sarah one of his megawatt smiles as she entered his one-room office in Burnt Cove village. "I thought you had gone back to Boston for the winter."

"It was just a visit. My ex was in an auto accident."

"I'm sorry to hear that. Is he okay?"

"He's better, thanks. He just needed a little help getting settled, physical therapy, and so on."

Brian nodded sympathetically. "Sometimes you just never seem to be done with an ex—at least that's the way it seems to be with mine."

He noticed Sarah's expression and quickly put on his professional face. "Your message said that you were looking for a place to rent for the winter?"

"Something on a lake would be nice. Something small, like a cabin, that doesn't need a lot of work."

"In the Burnt Cove area?"

"Yes, if possible."

"How soon would you like to move in? I have a place in mind, but it won't be available for another week. The owner hasn't cleaned it up yet."

"A week would be perfect," she replied, thinking that she'd have to stay with Oliver for a day or two anyway until he was settled. Or maybe a motel.

Brian pulled a sheet of paper from one of the folders on his desk and handed it to her. "Here's the place I'm thinking of. It's small, two bedrooms, full bath, common room, right on Pimm's Pond, about a mile up Squirrel Point road from Burnt Cove village. The pond isn't very big, a little over a mile long and half-a-mile wide, but there's a nice view, and the house is fully winterized, short driveway, private." He paused while Sarah read the information sheet.

Midcoast Maine was made up of a series of slender peninsulas, much like Squirrel Point, which had been gouged from the living rock by titanic glacial forces. These same forces had also carved slender ponds into some of the peninsulas.

"Could I see the place?" Sarah asked.

"We can run down there now, if you like. I've got the keys."

They covered the short distance in Brian's Volvo wagon, not noticing the nondescript rental which followed behind.

"A guy dropped into the office yesterday, asking about you," Brian said as they drove.

"Who would ask you about me?"

"It happens." Brian shrugged. "People figure the local Realtor knows everyone in town. He was young, maybe late twenties, skinny, and kind of hyper. He said his name was Vinnie. I can't remember the last name, but it was something Italian-sounding."

Sarah thought about the skinny kid who'd been standing beside the Tony Demano look-alike among SOCC's protesters this morning, and took a shot in the dark. "Demano?"

"Yes, that's it. Do you know him?"

"Not really," she said vaguely. "What did he want to know?"

"The usual stuff: how long you'd been here, where you lived, what you did, who your friends were." Brian turned to her. "Don't worry. I didn't tell him a thing, said I'd barely heard of you—the original tight-lipped Maine hick, that's me. He was some pissed off by the time he left. Of course, he could have been asking all over town about you."

Brian slowed. "Here's the driveway. It's a little steep down to the cabin, but it isn't too long and there's a place to park beside the road in the winter if you have to."

"A little steep" was an understatement. The driveway dropped precipitously to a cabin at the water's edge, and the building's rooftop seemed almost directly below Brian's Volvo.

———

The rental drove slowly by and stopped as the Volvo turned down a dirt driveway.

"What's up with this?" Vinnie said. "I thought that jerk said he barely knew Cassidy."

"Maybe she's buying another house," Sal said. "The guy's a

Realtor, after all."

"She's got her boyfriend living up the road, and a house in Massachusetts. How many places does she need?"

"Maybe this guy is another boyfriend," Sal suggested.

"And this is their love-nest," Vinnie added.

"Can't have too many of those."

"All I know," Vinnie grumbled, "is that following that broad around is driving me nuts."

Chapter 24 _____

Sal didn't understand the whole brandy-drinking thing from the word go. He watched Tony warming his after-dinner brandy goblet, or sniffer, or whatever it was called, in his hands, swirling a little bit of the booze around for a while before smelling it like he was afraid there might be a dead rat in there. Which made no sense, since there was nothing in the goblet but a few spoonfuls of brandy, which had enough alcohol in it to pickle a dead rat anyhow. Sal gave a mental shrug and followed Tony's example.

Sal had left Vinnie to trail after Cassidy, while he schlepped down to Boston for a late dinner and a meet with Tony, which wasn't all bad, since at least he'd be able to spend the night in his own bed for a change.

"I don't know what to make of the Cassidy woman, Uncle Tony," Sal said. "She and Dan Finlon were walking around Denton's woodlot this morning."

"Maybe she just wanted to look at the murder scene," Tony mused. "Morbid curiosity." Tony took a minute sip of the brandy. "Or maybe it's more than that. I don't like that she's getting together with Dan Finlon. I don't think he trusts us."

For good reason, Sal thought. "I figure old man Denton must have given her permission to go in there, and she asked Dan to show her around. His grandson sure as hell wouldn't have done that."

Tony nodded. "So she came up here from Boston and went right to the woodlot." He took another tiny sip of brandy. "Vinnie doing a good job of keeping an eye on her?"

"Mostly. He was asking about her around Burnt Cove. That's the town where she lives."

"You think that was smart?" Tony inquired.

The weight of family loyalty lay heavily on Sal's shoulders. He took a swig of his brandy before answering. "Vinnie's a good kid, but sometimes he gets a little—"

"Impetuous?" Tony suggested.

"Yeah. I keep telling him he needs to be more careful, more discrete, but sometimes he gets carried away and forgets."

Tony leaned back in his chair. "You're a good man, Salvatore. That's why I paired you up with Vinnie. You can teach him a lot, because he values your advice."

"Yes, Uncle Tony." Sal wasn't sure how Vinnie could value anybody's advice the way he kept going off on his own with some hair-brained idea.

"So what has Vinnie learned?" Tony said.

"Apparently she helped solve a double-murder last spring, and she and her boyfriend were involved in some kind of government thing in August. Bunch of people were killed."

Tony was leaning across the table now, his brandy forgotten. "The more I hear about this woman, the less I like it. Tell Vinnie to lay off the questions until I find out more about her. Maybe we should take her more seriously."

Sal nodded. "We have enough going on without somebody else poking around. You think she's some kind of private eye or undercover cop?"

"I think we need to be sure there aren't any loose ends lying around for her to trip over," Tony replied. He turned to his brandy. "I think you should call me right away if you need any more muscle. I don't want you and Vinnie doing any heavy stuff."

True to his word, Sal had called the building super, and the super, looking nervous and apologetic, turned up first thing Monday morning with a work crew in tow. Martha had gone home for the day to escape the noise and activity, and returned this morning to find the job done and sunlight flooding the room. For all Sal's faults, Martha Kirkland had to give him credit for getting things done, and the new window did a lot to brighten the space as well as Martha's mood.

She didn't have to like him, though.

Martha looked up from the papers on her desk. "There's a woodlot over in Gideon that I think we should look into," she said to Ken.

"That's a long way off," Ken said. "What's there?"

"A clearcut. There's a lot of cedar in that area, according to the surveys."

"Mmm," Ken said vaguely. "We're stretched pretty thin right now, what with the Denton lot. Let me talk to Sal and see what he thinks."

"Who's running this place anyway," Martha snapped, "you or Demano?"

"He's done SOCC a lot of good, Martha. Think about all the new members, the money, the new energy—"

"Not to mention new enemies and a broken window," she interjected.

"You can't make an omelet without—"

"Don't give me that crap. We're done with the Denton lot. The cedars are all cut. It's time to move on."

"They've made it personal by attacking our building—by attacking *us*," Ken said earnestly. "We can't let them push us around or nobody will take SOCC seriously any more. It's a matter of principle."

"I thought protecting the cedars was a matter of principle," she said. "What happened to our ideals? Why are you swallowing Sal's line of baloney?"

Ken looked at her stubbornly.

"Where is Sal anyway?" she added as an afterthought.

"He went down to Boston yesterday afternoon for a meeting of some kind. He should be back this afternoon."

Martha muttered under her breath.

"And I'm not swallowing his line," Ken added peevishly. "He's got good advice and I'm following it."

"Close your eyes and brush your fingers over it lightly," Oliver advised.

"Close my eyes?" Sarah said. "Are you sure about this? I feel like an idiot."

"Touch is more sensitive for finding bumps and hollows. People rely too much on their eyes, when their fingers often work better."

Sarah looked at Oliver's pale, drawn face. "You're just home from the hospital. Are you sure you should be out here doing this?"

"I've been lying around for days doing nothing. You want me to go stir crazy?"

Sarah sighed.

"Go ahead, close you eyes," Oliver prompted. "Did you know

that John Brown Herreshoff, the first of the Herreshoff yacht designing and building dynasty, went blind in his youth? That didn't stop him from becoming one of the most famous boat designers and builders of the late 1800's."

"Oh," Sarah said after a moment. "I see what you mean. There's a little ripple here on the hull."

Oliver beamed at her. "See how that works?" He was sitting, bundled up against the late afternoon chill, in a lawn chair which Sarah had brought into the boatshop. "You can skim a light across the surface and see the bigger bumps and hollows, but your fingers are a lot more sensitive to the smaller irregularities."

"It's a whole different perspective," she said, reaching for a sanding block.

"Just a few passes with the sandpaper will do it. A ripple like that might not show now, but it would stand out like sore thumb with a coat of glossy paint on the hull."

"Yes," Sarah replied thoughtfully, her fingers caressing *Daisy's* hull. "Maybe we need to do something like that with Carl Mueller's murder."

"Maybe we should forget about his murder."

"Ralph fired us yesterday morning."

Oliver straightened up in his chair. "Why did he do that?"

Sarah turned to face him. "Jack's crew were working in the woods, and I went in to talk. They didn't seem very happy to see me."

"You went in alone?"

"Why not?" Sarah bristled.

"Because maybe they're not as innocent as we think, that's why not."

"I thought we'd decided that Ralph was framed."

"Probably. Or maybe we've been thinking about Ralph the wrong way. Maybe we've been using our eyes when we should be using our fingers." Oliver zipped up his windbreaker as cool afternoon air drifted in through the open shop doors. "So what happened?" he added.

"I'm not sure, except I asked them about ATV trails. One of them runs near where Carl was killed."

"And you think it goes over to where Jack's crew is working?"

"It seems likely."

"So you asked about it and Ralph fired you? Not all that surprising, since an ATV trail would make Ralph's alibi a lot shakier."

"Of course," Sarah said, "but the police must know about those trails. Why didn't Ralph mention them to us when we first talked to him? How can we help him if he won't tell us the whole truth?"

"It sounds to me as though you were getting too close to the truth for comfort. Maybe Ralph decided you were going to end up doing him more harm than good, and that's why he fired you."

"Assuming I stay fired."

"What's the point in trying to help somebody who doesn't want help? We only went and talked to Ralph as a favor to Pearly, so he'd get his trees cut, remember? You're all done with that now, thanks to Ralph. Correction, *we're* all done now, so let's move on."

"It doesn't seem right to just walk away like that, even if Ralph doesn't want our help," she replied. "Besides, moving on may not be that easy."

"And why the hell not?"

"Remember the Tony Demano look-alike I told you about?"

"The guy who was with the SOCC picketers you photographed outside Ralph's house?" Oliver said.

Sarah nodded. "He had a younger man with him yesterday, on the picket line in front of Denton's woodlot. The two of them were standing a little apart from the rest of SOCC, talking to each other, and they seemed to recognize me."

"You didn't walk up and take his picture again, did you?"

"I was riding in Pastor Briskin's truck," she assured him. "The thing is, somebody who looks like this new guy—"

"The one talking to the Demano look-alike?"

"Who else? Pay attention. The thing is, he's been going around town asking about me, and his name is Vinnie Demano."

"Okay," Oliver said, "so you take a picture of some bozo outside Ralph's house, and this bozo might be named Demano, then you have a Tony Demano's car in your driveway, and now you've got a third Demano following you around? How many of these Demanos are chasing you anyway?"

Sarah frowned at Oliver. "Are you making fun of me?"

"Hell no," he replied solemnly. "I'm just trying to make sense of what you're saying, and I've decided that it's past time for a nap."

———

As it happened, a nap was not in the cards. Sarah, with some prompting from Oliver, had just gotten the livingroom wood stove going when Pearly knocked at the door.

"How's the patient?" Pearly said.

"Getting a little grumpy," Sarah replied.

"The patient is just fine," Oliver informed them.

"He tires easily," Sarah said.

"When was the last time you had a couple of gallons of blood drained out?" Oliver demanded.

"Yep, grumpy," Pearly said as he parked himself in front of the stove. "A little heat feels good. It's turning cold out there,"

"I just lit it," Sarah said with a hint of pride in her voice. "With a little help from Oliver," she added.

"She's a natural born firebug," Oliver commented.

"That's a good thing, from what I hear," Pearly said to Sarah, "now that you have a place of your own."

Oliver looked at Sarah. "A place of your own?"

The Burnt Cove gossip mill was even more efficient than Sarah had thought. "I told you I was going to do something like this. I just haven't gotten around to telling you that I *had* done it."

"Thanks for letting me know, Pearly," Oliver said.

Sarah sighed.

Sensing that he was in over his head, Pearly hurried on. "I thought you'd like to know that Pastor Briskin had a crash this morning. Lost his brakes and rolled the truck."

"Was he hurt?" Sarah said.

"I talked to him an hour ago and he's pretty banged up, but nothing too serious. Damn lucky it wasn't a lot worse."

"Coming back from Denton's woodlot?" Oliver said.

"Yes. On his way to Bucksport. It's hilly country in there."

"So he was fully loaded," Oliver said.

Pearly nodded. "The thing is," he said, "somebody had tampered with the brakes."

Sarah went pale. "Tampered with the brakes? When?"

"Most likely while he was waiting his turn to load up. He'd gone off to talk with Bruce and that's probably when somebody crawled underneath and crimped one of the lines so the brakes would fail when he stamped on them."

"Which would be likely on those hills," Oliver said. "Does he think someone from SOCC snuck in there and did it?"

"That's what he thinks. Of course it could have been any-body—it wouldn't have taken more than a few seconds to do the job with something like a pair of bolt cutters or lineman's pliers."

"I hope he's planning to turn the other cheek," Sarah said. "There are too many people out there looking for revenge as it is."

Pearly gazed at her for a second. "Funny you should put it that way. Did you know that if you strike someone with the back of your hand and he turns the other cheek, then you have to hit him with your palm, and that used to be a sign of respect? Think about it."

"What the hell are you talking about?" Oliver said.

"It sort of made sense when Briskin explained it." Pearly replied with a shrug. "Anyway, all I know is that he doesn't think about turning the other cheek the way we do. He's planning to bring out the entire Arms of Salvation Full Gospel church and have some kind of revival meeting at Denton's woodlot tomorrow."

"You've got to stop him, Pearly," Sarah said.

"Stop him? How? The man is a force of nature. Hell, I'm going out there and get some video."

"You don't understand. There are people in SOCC who are a lot more dangerous than Pastor Briskin realizes. Somebody could get killed out there."

"Somebody *did* get killed out there," Oliver murmured.

———

"Okay, so what's going on?" Sarah said after Pearly had left.

"What kind of tea is this?" Oliver inquired. He was sprawled on the livingroom sofa basking in the stove's warmth. It was a room he seldom used, a room filled with furniture his long-dead wife had selected when they lived in Boston.

"The healthy kind, for people who's blood is a few quarts low."

"Mmm," Oliver commented, taking a small sip. "I have a theory. One of many."

"Let's hear it."

"Okay, suppose Carl spiked the cedar tree—"

"Why?" Sarah asked.

"Because that's what SOCC does, protect cedar trees."

"But they've only found one spiked tree so far. Why just one tree?"

"Because the son-of-a-bitch was lazy, and pounding in those big spikes is hard work," Oliver replied sourly. "Then he sends an anonymous note to Young Derwin saying the trees are spiked—"

"Which Young Derwin ignores, the creep."

"Ah, but suppose he doesn't ignore the note after all," Oliver said. "Suppose he figures out that it's from Carl and decides to silence him, so he hires Ralph—"

Sarah cleared her throat.

"—or maybe Young Derwin kills Carl himself and frames Ralph for the murder by using his chainsaw—"

"Why drop a tree on Carl?"

"The tree thing is kind of weird," Oliver conceded, "but the point is that SOCC gets angry about Carl being squashed, so they picket Ralph because they've heard that his chainsaw was used."

"And they picket the cedar trees because Ralph helped cut them down?"

"That, and the fact they're cedar trees, which SOCC is in the business of protecting. Anyway, Pastor Briskin gives them a hard time on the picket lines, and makes Ken look like a fool—"

"Which isn't hard," Sarah commented.

"Not for Pastor Briskin. Naturally, Ken doesn't like being made to look like a fool, so he fiddles with Briskin's brakes to get back at him, and get him out of the way."

"Then who burned up the timber harvester?" Sarah said.

"That's a toughie," Oliver said, "but think about the time and money it will cost Bruce Nash to go over all those trees with a metal detector. Suppose he blamed Ken for the spikes and threatened him somehow—"

"And Ken trashed the harvester in retaliation?" Sarah said. "And Bruce shot up SOCC headquarters in retaliation for the timber harvester?"

"That's my theory, for what it's worth." Oliver took another sip of tea and grimaced.

"Your theory has an awful lot of bad guys."

"That's the trouble with feuds. Sooner or later everyone gets involved," Oliver said.

"A cycle of revenge," Sarah said.

"What worries me is that if my theory is true, then this isn't over yet," Oliver replied.

K en had spent the day brooding over Martha's remark about who was running SOCC, him or Sal. The question had particularly rankled because there could be an element of truth in it. Was Sal trying to take over the organization?

Carl's death had been tragic, of course, but Ken was an ambitious person and he'd thought of Carl's misfortune as an opportunity for himself. And for SOCC, naturally. The organization was pretty small potatoes, really, but with enough publicity Ken figured he could become a figure to be reckoned with in the state.

It had not occurred to him until now that Salvatore Demano might be planning to take over and stage a coup, so to speak.

Ken's mood wasn't improved by the letter in his hand, in which one of SOCC's pro bono lawyers expressed concern about the tree spiking business and Derwin Denton's possible lawsuit.

All these thoughts rattled around in Ken's brain as he sat at his desk, shuffling paperwork and watching Martha and two volunteers attaching handles to the signs. It was amazing how many were destroyed each time they went out. That bible-thumping trucker had mashed four of them all by himself yesterday. At least he wouldn't be bothering them tomorrow.

It was mid afternoon before Sal ambled in, looking rested, and all smiles and sweetness. Ken watched crossly as Sal admired the collection of signs. "Great work, gang," he said enthusiastically. "These look really good."

"I don't think we should picket the Denton lot anymore," Ken announced.

The room fell silent.

"What do you mean?" Sal said. "We're getting a lot of news coverage up there."

"But it's bad news coverage," Martha said. "It doesn't help our cause to be blamed—"

"*Any* press coverage that gets our name out there is good coverage," Sal retorted.

"There are more important things than press coverage," Ken said. "Our job is to protect the cedars. Carl found one stand of cedars on that woodlot before he was killed, but what if there are more—"

"Who cares if there are more?" Sal interrupted. "If there were some, that's enough. Besides, why waste time looking for cedar trees when we have bigger fish to fry?"

"Like what?" Martha demanded. "What's with you, anyway? All summer you were saying the Denton lot wasn't worth bothering with, and now you don't want us to move on."

"Carl's death changed everything," Sal replied. "Our mission has changed now," he added, thinking how true that statement was.

Martha's face went still.

"Look," Sal said, "the point is we that can't afford to abandon the work we've been doing on the Denton lot, especially where we're being blamed for that pulp truck accident. If we leave now, it'll look like we're admitting guilt."

"It wasn't an accident," Ken corrected him. *"Did* we have

anything to do with wrecking that pulp truck?"

"I can't imagine any of us doing a thing like that," Sal replied blandly.

"I'm not sure what some people's motives are around here," Ken muttered.

"There wasn't any cedar on the truck, was there?" Sal said.

"That's the whole point!" Martha yelled. "The cedar was already *gone!* We shouldn't be wasting our time there!"

Martha's outburst echoed through the room.

"Martha's right," Ken said. "We need to move on. That woodlot in Gideon looks promising to me."

"I've been studying the topographical map," Martha said, her anger spent, "and there's a brook running right across the lot. I want to find out how they plan to cut in there without polluting the water, especially where the there's a lot of wetlands nearby."

"We'll need to go up and see exactly where the good timber is," Ken added, excitement in his voice, "and where the access roads are likely to go."

Martha looked at Sal coldly. "This is what SOCC is all about," she said. The volunteers nodded agreement.

Sal scanned the rebellious room. "Of course this is what SOCC is all about," he said smoothly. "But to be effective, to have people listen to us, we've got to have respect. People have to know that we're serious. That we mean what we say. That we can't be pushed aside."

He held their gaze for a moment before going on. "I'll bet that whoever sabotaged that pulp truck was trying to destroy our reputation, like with the tree spiking. To intimidate us. To give us a bad name so people won't pay attention to our message."

Sal paused again for effect. "Don't you see? We can't slink away now, or it'll look like we're guilty of everything that's happened up there. We need to have one more day of picketing tomorrow, one last demonstration so we can go out with our heads held high."

Martha shook her head in disgust.

"One more day?" Ken said. "Just one?"

"We need to make one last statement of our commitment to the cedars of Maine."

"Bullshit," Martha muttered.

"You have the signs all made," Sal pointed out, "and I've got an idea that should make our demonstration even more effective."

"What idea," Ken said suspiciously.

"You remember when we picketed the other day and stood in the tote road?"

"And that pulp truck nearly ran us over?" Ken said.

"That was a mistake," Sal conceded, "and we ended up looking weak. I saw a pile of logs near where we were standing—"

"Four-foot, mixed hardwood," Martha commented.

"Whatever," Sal said. "I've got three strong friends lined up for tomorrow morning, first thing, and they'll move those logs across the tote road."

"You're going to block the tote road," Ken said flatly.

"Nobody will run us down tomorrow," Sal assured him.

"That's the dumbest thing I've heard all day," Martha said. "Do you think Bruce Nash and his crew are going to stand by and let you drag their logs around? They'll tear your friends to shreds."

"Nash and his crew will be a mile away in the woods," Sal pointed out.

"Not for long, they won't," Ken retorted.

"Don't you get it?" Sal said in exasperation, "we're making a statement, stopping the trucks—"

"And getting beaten up and arrested in the process," Martha said dryly. "Excuse me, but how does that help our reputation?"

"Nobody is going to get beaten up," Sal assured her.

"Your 'strong' friends are going to make sure of that?" Ken said sarcastically. "Have they seen Nash's crew?"

"This is a photo-op, for chrissake. For publicity," Sal exclaimed. "We'll wait until his crew is off working before we put up the barricade. All we're going to do is stop the pulp trucks long enough to get some news coverage, take the logs out of the road, and go home."

"And nobody's going to get hurt?" Ken said dubiously.

"Absolutely not," Sal assured him. "It'll be a piece of cake."

———————

The Friendly's restaurant on Augusta's Western Avenue didn't serve three-hundred-dollar bottles of wine, like the places Tony frequented, but Sal wasn't in the mood for ritzy food after his experience at SOCC headquarters.

"That damn Martha Kirkland gives me a pain," Sal muttered as he brooded over his Patty Melt.

"Sounds like she put some backbone into Ken," Vinnie replied sympathetically. "He's never given you trouble before, has he?"

"Hell no. He's been a lot easier than Carl Mueller ever was. Until this afternoon."

"You sure got yourself in a box," Vinnie mused as he popped a couple of French Fries into his mouth.

Sal glared at his companion.

"The good thing," Vinnie added hastily, "is that you can get out of here in another week or so."

"I'm not sure SOCC will stay in line that long, thanks to Kirkland," Sal said morosely.

"Why should we care anymore? Why don't you just let them go off to this other woodlot and picket there?"

Sal thought about this for a moment. "I would," he replied, "except I don't trust Ken anymore. The guy said some things this afternoon that got me worried."

"Damned ingrates, after all the money you pumped into their half-assed organization."

"I'll be glad to see the last of them, that's for sure," Sal said.

"Why don't you ask The Thumb to send up some muscle? You know, lean on Ken a little. Make him understand what his best interests are."

"Are you nuts?" Sal retorted.

"Or they could lean on Kirkland, rough her up a little bit. After all, she's the one who's stirring up Ken."

"Jesus," Sal snarled. "The last thing I need is a bunch of goons wandering around town roughing people up. Especially SOCC. Too many people are watching those clowns as it is."

"But you've already—"

"The hell with SOCC. We need to work some other angles."

"You've put a lot of time and money into them," Vinnie pointed out.

"We got our money's worth. You know what Tony says—"

"Take your winnings and walk away while you're ahead?" Vinnie suggested.

"You got it." Sal thought for a moment. "What about Cassidy? Where is she?"

"Looks like she's planning to spend the night with her boyfriend. At least that's where she was when I left off tailing her," Vinnie replied. "She brought him home from the hospital this afternoon."

Sal nodded to himself as he thought about Cassidy, and about another one of Tony The Thumb's helpful sayings: "Always turn a problem into a solution."

Chapter 26

They left early Wednesday morning, taking Sarah's Ford Explorer, since it was the only vehicle that would hold the four of them. Oliver sat in front looking pale and anemic, while Pearly and Eldon sat in the rear.

They arrived at Denton's woodlot little after seven o'clock and parked at the pavement's edge. The air was cool and raw, the sky an iron gray when they got out of the SUV, and Sarah put on her fleece jacket. A group of SOCC protesters were waving placards across from the tote road leading into Denton's woodlot.

A TV news van was unloading their equipment nearby, and Sarah could hear a chorus of machinery in the distance—Bruce Nash's crew already hard at work.

"I don't see Briskin's bunch yet," Pearly commented.

"They have to come all the way up from Damariscotta," Eldon replied.

The roar of a pulp truck laboring up the hill assailed their ears.

Suddenly, a group of men broke away from the picketers and

dashed across the road, while the rest followed more slowly.

"What are they up to?" Pearly wondered.

"One way to find out," Oliver said, walking briskly towards the tote road.

By the time they got there, the men had looted a stack of four-foot logs and constructed a substantial barricade across the tote road. The rest of the picketers, under Ken Poirier's guidance, stationed themselves behind the logs, where they waved their signs and chanted as though fending off a barbarian horde.

The pulp truck began its turn off the pavement, stopped with a lurch well back from the protesters' roadblock, and blew a blast from its horn. The driver reached for a microphone, which was hanging beside the sun visor, and began talking into it.

"I don't like the look of this," Pearly muttered.

"Where are the cops?" Eldon said.

The distant machinery became silent.

"This could get messy," Oliver murmured.

With the rear end of the pulp truck sticking out onto the pavement, and assorted cars parked on the verges, the narrow, two-lane road was becoming congested. The resulting back-up, not to mention the TV news van, collected a growing number of onlookers who abandoned their cars to see what was happening.

Sarah wondered how Pastor Briskin would deal with the situation when he got here.

It didn't take long to find out, for a large, sky-blue van with the words, "Arms of Salvation Full Gospel Church" on its side, pulled up behind the pulp truck. A dozen people dismounted and surged towards the barricade with Pastor Briskin hobbling along in the lead, bible in one hand, crutch in the other.

"Hallelujahs!" filled the air.

Pearly pulled a camcorder out of his pocket and trotted happily after Briskin's flock. "This will be a story for my grandchildren someday," he said.

"Somebody is going to get killed," Oliver muttered.

Unstoppable as the incoming tide, Pastor Briskin's followers streamed up the tote road and stationed themselves between the pulp truck and the barricade, nose-to-nose with SOCC's picketers.

Sarah hung back as her two companions moved forward for a better view of the two groups as they traded slogans while waving bibles and placards in the air.

From where she stood at the pavement's edge, the confrontation seemed to be all noise and gestures, but no violence.

So far.

Sarah noticed a familiar figure advancing on the picketers. Young Derwin Denton shook his fist and shouted threats as he neared the picket line, and was shouted at in return. Did he live around here? Had he driven all the way up from Yarmouth?

Sarah hoped the police would get here soon. Really soon. Meanwhile, TV cameras ate up the scene, which would undoubtably be featured on the evening news.

Sarah turned and saw a familiar-looking woman standing alone a few steps away.

"Aren't you a member of SOCC?" Sarah said, walking over to the woman. "Weren't you picketing Ralph Barne's house last week?"

The woman looked at Sarah for a second. "You took our picture up there. You sure bugged the hell out of Sal. I guess that means you can't be all bad." She held out her hand. "I'm Martha Kirkland."

"Sarah Cassidy," Sarah replied. "I didn't realize you had so many members."

"We don't," Martha said. "Sal hired those three tough-looking apes for the morning. I saw him slip each of them a hundred-dollar bill when he thought I wasn't looking. He likes to make a big show."

"Why aren't you on the picket line today?"

"This is just making trouble for the sake of making trouble, as far as I'm concerned," Martha said tartly. She glowered at the noisy mob, as it sang hymns and traded threats. "Great, Derwin is all we need. Sal will be pleased to have him around, yelling and shaking his fist at everybody." Martha turned away in disgust. "Good publicity," she added bitterly.

"Surely Derwin can't have known about this ahead of time, or he'd have warned Bruce and called the police long ago."

"It's probably pure, dumb luck that Derwin is here. He's been coming up every day or so to see how things are going." Martha stared angrily at the mob. "Look at Sal's goddamn circus. This has nothing to do with SOCC, or its mission."

"Then why are you here?"

Martha gave her an impatient look. Apparently deciding not to answer, she said, "This is all Sal Demano's lame-brained idea. Sal, the little Mussolini, thinks he's running SOCC, though I don't see him over there now." She scanned the crowd with a scowl. "Typical of him. Do you know Sal?"

"As little as possible," Sarah replied vaguely.

"Smart of you."

"Has he been with SOCC for long?"

"Too long. He turned up this spring, and things have been going to hell ever since."

"Like Carl Mueller's death?"

Martha's face seemed to crumple.

"I'm sorry," Sarah said gently. She impulsively reached out, touching Martha's arm.

"You really want to know why I came here today?" Martha said, wiping her eyes impatiently. "I want to see the place where he died. It sounds silly, but I do."

The roar of an approaching skidder reached Sarah's ears. Nash's crew. "I hope the police get here soon."

"I've called them twice already," Martha said, worry in her voice, "but I suppose with all this traffic. . ."

One of the tree felling machines, bristling with angry loggers, came bouncing and lurching down the tote road at a breakneck speed and pulled up behind the chanting, singing, praying, swearing groups confronting each other across the barricade. This might be Pastor Briskin's idea of a revival, Sarah mused, but she doubted if he was making any converts.

Taken aback by the scene, the loggers paused uncertainly for a moment before wading in.

"Dan Finlon took me there," Sarah said. "To where Carl died."

Martha looked at her.

"I could take you to the place if you like. Derwin Denton gave me permission to go on his land."

The loggers were well in amongst the picketers now, pushing and shoving as they struggled to drag logs out of the tote road. Pastor Briskin had wisely moved his congregation to a safer spot beside the tote road, where they began a rousing version of *The Old Rugged Cross.*

"I can find it myself," Martha replied.

"It's a track on the right, where the tote road bears left beyond the ATV trail."

"Beyond the ATV trail?" Martha was quiet for a while as she watched the action at SOCC's barricade.

"I was hoping to sneak away this morning and go in there," Martha said, "but the way things look now, there's no chance to get by that crowd."

Inevitably, a punch was thrown as a logger tried to pull a log from the roadblock. Sarah was relieved to see Oliver, Pearly, and Eldon backing away from the rapidly developing melee.

"Is the place far from the tote road?" Martha asked.

"A couple of minutes."

The distant sound of a siren greeted their ears.

Martha studied Sarah's face. "I've kind of dreaded sneaking in for fear of being caught by Nash and his crew. I don't imagine they'd be too pleased to find the vice-president of SOCC wandering around in there, considering all the hard feelings. On the other hand, if you have permission from Derwin and were with me—"

"Tomorrow morning?"

The onlookers' cars began to move out on as the siren grew nearer.

"Ten o'clock?" Martha said. She paused and added, "I can meet you at Denny's out by the Augusta mall."

"I'll be there," Sarah replied, feeling a mixture of anticipation at the chance to learn more about what SOCC was up to, and fear of what she might learn.

A pair of State Police cruisers pulled up to the scene and disgorged their occupants, who took one look at the dozen men fighting over a pile of logs, while another group sang *Meet Me at the River* a few yards away, and called for backup before advancing on the mob.

———

Martha took one look at the cruisers, climbed into her car and left, figuring that Ken and Sal had created this mess and could damn well could fend for themselves. If they managed to run off into the woods and elude capture, that was okay, otherwise Sal would just have to put up the bail. Bruce Nash was the only one she felt sorry for, since he was going to loose another day's work.

Martha was soon followed by the Arms of Salvation Full Gospel Church van, Sarah and her companions, and the last gawkers.

A few of those who had been battling over the barricade escaped into the woods, but most were rounded up and escorted away by the police. Ken was among the missing.

———————

Ken was still stewing over Martha's outburst of yesterday. The problem was that both Martha and Sal had good points. On the one hand, SOCC's recent activism, aided and abetted by Sal, had generated a lot of publicity and new members. But Martha was right too. All the picketing was distracting them from SOCC's primary goal of protecting the forest—especially the cedars—from exploitation.

The more Ken fussed over this, the more he became convinced of the need to return, at least partly, to their founding purpose.

And so, while the confrontation at the barricade played itself out, Ken tramped through the woods to complete the search for cedars which Carl had begun.

Chapter 27 _____

As often happens on a mid-September day in Maine, Wednesday's cool, gray morning gave way to a warm, sunny afternoon.

"What a beautiful Indian Summer afternoon," Sarah exclaimed as *Owl* ghosted along on a light Northerly breeze. Burnt Cove opened into Kwiguigum Sound, and they were tacking up the sound towards the upper end where it narrowed into a tidal creek. The rocky shore here was lined with summer houses, many of which were already closed up for the winter.

"Technically speaking," Oliver replied, "it's not really Indian Summer."

"And why is that, pray tell?"

"We haven't had a frost yet. No frost, no Indian Summer."

"You're a hell of a nit-picker," Sarah retorted. "I should have left you home and just brought Wes."

Wes, hearing his name, wagged happily from his spot on the seat beside Oliver.

"Seriously," Sarah added, "are you sure you aren't doing too much? I mean you were in a near riot this morning and now sailing in the afternoon. That's a lot for someone just out of the hospital."

"I wasn't *in* a near riot, I was just *watching* a near riot. There's a big difference. Besides," he went on somberly, "September always reminds me how fast time goes by, and life is short, so we should enjoy it while we can."

"Thanks for those cheery words, but you have to admit it's a glorious afternoon." She gave a contented sigh. "You know, I've never sailed this time of year."

"Really? What kind of deprived childhood did you have?"

"I grew up in Boston, remember? The only sailing I did before this year was when I was a kid at camp Migawoc, and we were done by mid-August."

"You've missed something, then. September and October are two of the best months to be on the water. On Indian Summer days like this—" Sarah punched his arm playfully, "—the air is clear, the trees are turning," he went on dreamily.

Oliver turned to Sarah. "I saw you talking to one of the SOCC people at the riot."

"Martha Kirkland. She's the vice-president of SOCC, now that Carl is dead. I think she may have been Carl Mueller's girlfriend. She seemed pretty upset about his death." Sarah was tempted to mention tomorrow's date with Martha, but thought better of it. Why get Oliver upset over nothing?

"Must be hard for her," he commented.

"She doesn't like Sal Demano."

"Fine, but did she tell you for sure if this Sal Demano character is connected to the Tony Demano mobster who was stalking your house?"

"All I know is that Sal Demano has only been around since spring and comes from Boston, according to Martha, and she blames him for most of the shenanigans that SOCC has been up to lately."

"I thought Ken Poirier was running SOCC," Oliver said.

"Martha gave me the impression that Sal is manipulating Ken, and she doesn't approve."

Oliver nodded. "Ken doesn't strike me as being the brightest bulb on the marquee. So why wasn't Martha manning the picket line today?"

"She doesn't approve of the kind of picketing where people get arrested, run over by pulp trucks, or beaten up. Apparently Sal hired three of the thugs who were out there this morning, at a hundred bucks a head, to help build the barricade."

They were working their way towards the head of the sound now, tacking into the wind in ever shorter legs as the shorelines converged. The cottages here were smaller and older, unlike the new, oversized mansions further out. Most of the trees here were fir and spruce, but the tops of a stand of swamp maple, already turning a brilliant red, could be seen a hundred yards inland.

"That's a lot of money just to hire a bunch of muscle to move some logs," Oliver commented.

"And start a fight with Bruce Nash and his crew," Sarah added.

"An interesting point," Oliver said thoughtfully. "It certainly looks like Ken, or Sal, or both of them, have a grudge against Bruce Nash."

"I can understand why Bruce is mad at SOCC, what with all the trouble they've caused him, but why the other way around?"

"Maybe SOCC hates loggers in general," Oliver suggested. "After all, it's the loggers of the world who are cutting down all of SOCC's cedars."

"SOCC's cedars? Dan doesn't think there's a shortage of cedars in Maine."

"He should know," Oliver said.

"Is SOCC just manufacturing a crisis so they can profit from it, then, or are they sincere?"

"A Cause without a cause?" Oliver mused. "Interesting. Idle hands are the devil's workmen, as they say."

"Martha seems to think their cause is real, and she strikes me as being pretty level headed."

"If a person really believes in something, even if it isn't real," Oliver commented, "that person can bring along a lot of followers."

"Real cause or not, there's more to SOCC than meets the eye," Sarah said, hoping tomorrow's excursion with Martha would give her some more insight into the group's operation. Obviously they did some picketing, and according to Martha, took legal action against illegal timber cutting, but what else did they do?

"Everything that's happened seems to revolve around SOCC," Oliver said, "except Ralph and his chainsaw."

"What about his chainsaw?"

"Why try to frame Ralph? Why pick on him?"

"The saw was just lying there in his truck, and somebody had to be framed," Sarah pointed out.

"So it was just bad luck that his saw was used?"

"Why not?"

Oliver sighed. "I can't help thinking that Ralph knows something, and that's why he was framed—if he was framed. He did fire us, after all."

Sarah had a strategically folded chart on the seat beside her, and she glanced at the thickening collection of asterisks—which were, of course, rocks lurking below the surface.

"Shouldn't we turn around before we run into something?" she said.

"Hug the shore to the left and you'll be fine. The rocks are in the middle here," he said casually. "Have you ever sailed into Lowe's Cove? The wind and tide are just right for us to stick our noses in there."

Lowe's Cove lay just ahead—a narrow break in the rocky

shoreline, barely thirty feet wide at its mouth. "I thought it was too small for anything bigger than a rowboat," Sarah said, looking at the chart doubtfully.

"It's fine on a day like this when the tide is high and the wind is light. And you're careful."

"If my boat lands on a rock, it'll be your fault."

"Orient your chart," Oliver said. "Less chance of getting turned around."

Sarah rotated the chart so it faced the direction they were heading.

"Big rock smack in the middle," Sarah murmured as they glided through the narrow opening. She hugged the right-hand side, starboard, she reminded herself, avoiding the obstacle.

"The cove is a lot bigger than it looks on the chart, once you get inside it," Sarah said. It was, she realized, nearly a hundred yards long, and half that in width, strewn with boulders—some above, but most below the surface. Four small boats were moored down the middle of the cove.

Sarah eyed the chart while Oliver stared into the glassy water ahead, pointing to submerged rocks. Wes stood on the seat, leaned over the rail, and stared into the water as well, trying to see what Oliver was looking at and hoping it was something he could fetch.

"This is really beautiful, so still and quiet," she commented, gazing at the marsh grass, sprinkled with huge boulders, which lined the cove's sides. A small, weathered one-roomed cabin perched on one of the boulders from where it looked down on the glassy, blue-green water. The placid quiet, broken only by the occasional call of a gull over the sound, made a welcome respite after the morning's turmoil.

Mesmerized by the stillness, Sarah let *Owl* glide as far as she dared to head of the cove before turning around.

She dutifully reoriented the chart when they tacked, wanting to make sure she didn't turn the wrong way around one of the rocks as she zig-zagged between them—

"We need to reorient our chart," she said abruptly.

"You just did."

"I mean our mental chart of Ralph and SOCC, and what's going on."

"To avoid running onto a metaphorical SOCC rock?"

"Cute, but maybe we've already run onto a SOCC rock. I think we need to look at our basic assumptions. Maybe they're all wrong. Maybe Carl's murder isn't about SOCC and its activities. Maybe there's something else going on, and SOCC is just a distraction."

"That's possible," Oliver mused. "Maybe it's not a chain of revenge, a feud, like the Hatfields and McCoys. Maybe it's a magician's trick."

"Okay, now you're babbling."

"Think about everything that's happened: Carl's murder, SOCC's picketing, the tree spiking, the timber harvester burning, pulp truck wrecking, this morning's battle at the barricade. What if they're all just distractions to take our eyes off what's really happening."

"So who is the magician, then?" Sarah said.

"The one who is hiding something."

"That's not a big help."

Oliver looked at her solemnly. "We need to be careful not to get so busy watching one rock that we end up hitting a bigger one."

"Speaking of Ralph and hiding things, the more questions I asked Jack's crew when I dropped in on them, the more nervous they got."

"Could just be that they're men," Oliver said, stating the obvious. "Maybe they were uncomfortable having a woman traipsing into the woods and talking to them all by herself."

"So, you think they're just male chauvinists who fired me because they discovered that I'm a woman?"

Oliver shrugged. "All I'm saying is that there could be other reasons for them being nervous, besides Ralph's chainsaw."

"A minute ago you were suggesting that Ralph, or maybe all three of them, were involved in killing Carl, and now you're suggesting they're just clueless MCP's. Who's side are you on?"

"The more I think about all this, the happier I am that we were fired," Oliver said placidly, "and I think we should take the hint and forget about this whole business."

Sarah frowned, glad now that she hadn't mentioned tomorrow's rendezvous with Martha.

Chapter 28

Sarah drove up with Martha in her Prius, parking on the shoulder of the road well away from the access road into Denton's woodlot.

"We can cut into the woods right here," Martha said as the got out.

"I know the way from the tote road, but I'm not sure about getting there from here," Sarah said.

"It doesn't matter. I've got the woodlot on my GPS, so we can just go parallel to the tote road until we to hit your path to the spot. Besides, I don't want to take a chance of running into one of Nash's crew. You may have permission to walk around in there, but they might not be so happy to see me. Not after all the grief Ken has been giving them."

Martha pulled a small backpack from the rear seat and rummaged through it, extracting a revolver.

"What's that for?" Sarah said, alarmed.

"My little Saturday Night Special? I just like to carry something when I'm off in the woods," Martha said casually, as she put the weapon in the pocket of her jeans. "It's only a .25 caliber, wouldn't stop a bear, but you never know when a gun might come in handy out here."

"Do you know how to use it?"

"Of course. I grew up in Maine." Martha shouldered the backpack, stepped across a roadside ditch, and headed for the trees. "Looks like an old game trail right here," she said over her shoulder.

"Next to that 'No Trespassing' sign?"

"You brought the note from Derwin Denton, didn't you?" Martha said.

"Of course."

"Let's go then," Martha replied with a smile as she slipped through an opening in the brush.

It was heavy going at first, as they worked their way single-file through thick brush and soggy ground, but soon they were on higher land among larger trees where the walking was easier.

"Did Carl have permission from Derwin to be in here?" Sarah asked.

Martha laughed. "Derwin Denton give the president of SOCC permission to go on his land? Of course not." She paused to consult her GPS. "But there's always a way to get onto a piece of posted land like this without actually seeing a no trespassing sign."

"You mean sneak in where there aren't any signs?"

Martha gave Sarah a sly smile. "It's not possible to post every foot of a parcel of land this size, and Carl could be a little nearsighted at times."

"See no sign, as in the three monkeys?"

"Something like that," Martha replied as she set off again.

After tramping along on in silence for a while, Sarah said, "How do you find woodlots to investigate, if that's the right word?"

"Anybody planning to harvest a woodlot commercially has to file a 'Forest Operation Notification' form with the state and the local town. The form tells us where the woodlot is, its rough size, and so on. Then we pick out the promising ones to investigate."

"Investigate? What do you do besides picket them?"

"Our real work has nothing to do with waving signs, and it's a lot more than just protecting cedars; it's about protecting the whole forest in general," Martha replied earnestly. "As I said, we look for woodlots that are about to be cut over, review the applications, walk over the land—like Carl was doing when he was killed—to look for areas that could be damaged by wood cutting. Areas like brooks, swamps, and so forth that will need protection. We also monitor the work as it goes along to make sure the clear-cut regulations are being followed—"

"Even if it means trespassing?"

Martha stopped abruptly to glare at Sarah. "Some things are more important than a few no trespassing signs. People like Bruce Nash, or your friend Jack Fournier, will cut corners to save time and money. The state doesn't have the manpower to watch over it all, so it's up to us to help protect the forest."

"Some people don't seem to appreciate your efforts."

"That's their problem." Martha strode on. "Ken and Sal, with their damn picketing, are a travesty of our real mission. Carl understood. He truly believed in his work."

Martha stopped again, turning to Sarah. "Do you know how vital cedar trees are to the forest? Not just the big trees, but the saplings that provide browse and bedding for the deer and who knows how many small animals. Cedars are being stripped from the landscape to make lawn furniture and porches with no attention to the real cost. People will tell you there are lots of cedars in Maine today, and they're right, at least partly, but what about the larger trees? What about tomorrow? We can't keep stripping the land forever. Sal doesn't begin to understand, or care. For him it's just about money and building a reputation."

Martha caught herself, sighed. "Sorry, but I get so frustrated sometimes. . ."

"Sal and Ken must have been pleased with yesterday's ruckus, then."

"I haven't seen either of them since yesterday. They may still be in jail for all I care." Martha turned on her heal and forged ahead.

———————

"You'll never guess where Cassidy is now," Vinnie said into his cell. "I followed her and Kirkland up to Denton's woodlot."

"The two of them are together?" Sal said.

"Damn right. I almost lost Cassidy. She met up with Martha at Denny's, and they took Martha's car.

"Martha's car?"

"Yeah. You know, that little roller skate she drives. Gets a gazillion miles to the gallon."

"I know the goddam car, Vinnie. But why did Cassidy swap off like that? Does she know you're following her?"

"Not a chance. I've been trading rentals every coupla days," Vinnie replied, sounding hurt. "Martha probably insisted. You know how she boasts about that thing."

Sal wondered what this turn of events meant. Nothing good, he bet. It had never occurred to him that the two women might get together, maybe compare notes. After all, they'd been on opposite sides when SOCC was picketing Ralph Barnes. "What are they doing now?" he said.

"Last I saw, they were going off into the woods, not too far from Nash's logging road," Vinnie replied. "I had to drive a mile up the road to get you on my cell—lousy coverage around here. And don't ask me to go back and follow them, because I'm not going into any woods, not with all those wild animals, deer ticks, bears, and all that stuff. No way I want to get bit by some goddam rabid moose."

"Jesus, Vinnie, the last thing I want is to have you wandering around those woods. I want you to stay there, and keep an eye on the car in case they come back. I'll make a call, just to be on the safe side."

"With that backpack Kirkland was carrying, it didn't look like they were planning to come back anytime soon."

The more Sal thought about the situation, the more he figured that things could work out well if he played his cards right.

"We must be getting close," Sarah said. "We crossed the ATV trail a while ago, and it seems like we've gone a long way since then."

"It just seems far because we're plowing through the underbrush instead of going on the logging road," Martha said curtly. "We've got a way to go yet."

"Are you sure? I don't remember it as being—"

Martha turned on Sarah. "Do you think I'm an idiot? I've studied topographical maps and satellite photographs of this lot until I'm blue in the face."

Martha waved her GPS under Sarah's nose.

"We are right here!" Martha's finger stabbed at the GPS. "See that 'X' mark? That's where Carl was murdered! We're a long way from the spot." The GPS quivered in Martha's hands.

Sarah stepped back, suddenly aware of Martha's size and muscular build. How could Martha be so sure where Carl had died?

As though to underscore Sarah's alarm, a nearby crow, startled by the intruders, sounded a warning call. Great, Sarah though to herself, this is turning into something out of Edgar Allen Poe.

After a second, Martha let out a shaky sigh, adding in a subdued voice, "I'm sorry about blowing up like that, but this is being a lot harder than I thought it would."

"Why don't we keep going then?" Sarah said, trying to placate her volatile companion.

She was reassured to hear the sound of a pulp truck not far to her left. At least they were close to the logging road.

Suddenly, they were crossing a narrow, freshly-cut trail. Sarah stopped in her tracks, saying, "This is it. This is the trail the police made to reach the murder scene."

"Can't be," Martha retorted. "The spot is way up ahead."

"It's a hundred feet off the right," Sarah snapped, angry at Martha's stubbornness.

"One woods trail can look like any other," Martha pointed out.

"Humor me," Sarah replied tartly. Not waiting for a response, Sarah headed down the trail. Martha heaved a sigh and followed.

It was more than a hundred feet, and Sarah was beginning to think Martha had been right after all, when they came into the clearing.

"This is it," Sarah said triumphantly.

Martha stood for a moment, transfixed. "He was killed with a dead tree," she said at last in a small voice.

Sarah didn't see why the tree made any difference, but the grief-stricken woman moved away before Sarah could think of a way to frame the question tactfully.

Sarah hung back as Martha advanced on the tree and touched its shattered crown as though trying to feel some hint Carl's last life-breath in the dry, brittle wood.

Watching her companion's grief, Sarah concluded that Martha might be a stubborn, opinionated idealist, but she wasn't a killer—at least not of Carl Mueller.

Martha slowly walked down the tree trunk in some kind sad communion that Sarah didn't dare interrupt.

Martha came at last to the place where a piece of the trunk had been cut away to free Carl's body, and paused. From where she stood, Sarah could see where Carl's blood had soaked into the shallow ground.

Just then, Martha screamed.

Chapter 29 _____

Athena was a big boat. It wasn't her forty-foot length or towering mast so much as her width and height that made *Athena* so bulky. She was tied up to Burnt Cove's town pier, and about to be hauled out of the water by Cassie Greene's boat hauler. After that, *Athena* would travel to Pearly's yard where the sixty-year-old vessel would have a couple of punky frames replaced.

Cassie had backed the trailer part of her big rig into the water on a long cable, so the trailer's four arms were all that jutted up above the surface to hold *Athena* in their hydraulic embrace. Or so Pearly fervently hoped.

The problem was that Wednesday's high pressure system, with its gentle northerlies, had moved offshore during the night, bringing a cool, gusty southeast wind for Thursday morning. Although Burnt Cove was a small harbor, perhaps four hundred yards across, and well sheltered from most directions, it was exposed to the southeast.

Because of that wind, *Athena* didn't want to be embraced by Cassie's boat hauler. Pearly stood on the pier, holding a long line that led to the boat's bow, while Cassie's assistant, a weedy-looking kid in his late teens, stood beside the truck with a second line.

From his vantage point, Pearly had a good view down to the launching ramp below, and he watched as Cassie, a control box on a long cable in her hands, pushed a few buttons to readjust the arms and nodded up to Pearly.

"Try it again!" Pearly shouted to Eldon, who was stationed in *Athena's* cockpit, since the owner had prudently returned to Baltimore for the winter.

With a rumble of her engine, the boat eased forward, perfectly aligned with the trailer.

"That's good, keep her coming!" Cassie yelled.

Pearly backed up the pier, keeping his line taut, while Cassie's assistant did the same from his side.

Just as *Athena's* bow nuzzled between the first two arms, a gust of wind caught her. The problem with the damn boat, Pearly reflected, was that she had too much freeboard, and all that height above the water turned her topsides into sail which caught every puff of wind that came along.

As it had twice before, the boat twisted out of position. Pearly heaved on the line and wondered why Eldon wasn't up here wrestling with this great, white pig. *Moby Dick* would have been a better name for the damn boat, in which case he was Ahab, but without the harpoon.

Pearly heaved against *Athena's* twenty-thousand pounds of ornery, wind-driven weight and wished he had a harpoon—one of those cannon-fired jobs with an explosive head.

"Need a hand?"

Pearly glanced over his shoulder and saw Jack Fournier, BB Pearson, and Ralph Barnes grinning at him.

"What does it look like, you goddamn fools?" Pearly growled. With the four of them pulling, *Athena* reluctantly straightened and slid into place.

"Jeez," BB commented, "that's a big 'un. You work harder than I figured."

"Why aren't you off somewhere, knocking down trees?" Pearly inquired.

"We wanted to talk," Jack replied.

Pearly glanced down at Cassie. Her blond pigtail, sprouting from a gimmie cap, swayed as she moved back and forth, checking and adjusting the arms with her control box.

"So talk, but make it quick," Pearly said gruffly. "I've got to get that boat over to my yard."

Cassie, satisfied that *Moby Dick* was finally subdued and secure on the trailer, engaged the big winch mounted behind the truck's cab and the boat slowly crept out of the water.

"We're gettin' worried about having your friends help Ralph," Jack said.

Pearly watched as the trailer latched onto the truck with a clank, and silently counted to ten before replying.

"I went to a lot of trouble getting them to help you," he growled, "because you pestered me to do it. Now you're telling them to buzz of, and you won't even answer Sarah's questions. That doesn't look good for Ralph."

"Just don't want them getting hurt," Ralph muttered.

With a roar, the hauler eased up the ramp onto level ground. Eldon was watching Pearly form *Athena's* cockpit. Pearly shook his head fractionally.

"Tell me again," Pearly demanded, "and no bullshit this time: did you have anything to do with Carl Mueller's death?"

"No," Ralph moaned. "I never killed anybody. We just don't want her gettin' hurt."

Pearly leaned into Ralph's personal space, which smelled of fir, spruce, and sweat. "And why would having Sarah ask *you* questions get *her* hurt? What the hell are you clowns trying to hide?"

"We ain't trying to hid anything, 'least not exactly," Jack said. "It's just that the cops haven't been around pestering Ralph for a while, so we—"

"You're kidding, right?" Pearly said. "You know perfectly well that just because the cops aren't on Ralph's case right now doesn't mean he's off the hook. They're just digging up more evidence. And all this waffling makes you look guilty as hell. Jesus, even I'm beginning to wonder."

Pearly paused, watched Cassie set up an extension ladder and climb aboard *Athena* to help Eldon unhook the rigging so the mast could be taken out.

"It's not like that," Ralph said. "It's just that things are going on up there—"

"You mean like people being killed, machinery torched, stuff like that?" Pearly retorted. "Did it occur to you that you have a responsibility to tell the cops what you know? Whatever the hell that might be?"

Pearly saw Cassie's assistant backing a crane truck alongside *Athena*. The mast would be out of her soon, and all they'd have to do would be to lash everything down for the thirty-minute trip to Pearly's yard. Eldon was shooting curious glances at the group on the pier, and Pearly mentally scolded him to concentrate on what he was doing, and for god's sake not drop the mast through the bottom of the boat.

"Things could go real bad for us if we try to put the law on them," Jack said.

"There's three of them, real tough people," BB added.

"All the more reason to tell the cops and put them away, whoever they are," Pearly replied. "I can't believe we're having this conversation."

"You don't understand," Ralph said.

"*What* don't I understand?" Pearly demanded. "Jesus! Talking to you is like kicking a bunch of skunks!"

Eldon and Cassie looked up, startled by Pearly's outburst. Pearly pointed urgently at the mast, which was swinging precariously over Eldon's head.

Jack sighed. "It's those ATVs," he said. Ralph and BB looked at him nervously.

"What about them?" Pearly prompted.

"We've heard them coming through every day, about a mile in from were we've been cutting."

"Every afternoon," BB added.

"So what?" Pearly said. "I thought kids ran through those woods all the time."

"That regular?" Jack retorted. "Hell, ain't you thinking at all? It can only mean one thing. Somebody's growing pot back there in the puckerbrush somewheres."

"All this is about pot?" Pearly said.

"They must be goin' in every afternoon to cover the plants," Jack explained. "Makes them think the days are gettin' short. Fools them into blooming quicker, before the frost hits 'em. It's the flowers that's got the best stuff."

Pearly wondered how Jack knew so much about growing pot, but didn't ask.

"It's hard growin' pot out of door in Maine," Jack went on. "I imagine they'll be hauling the stuff out in a week or less, maybe even now."

Pearly watched the mast and boom being stowed on the trailer alongside *Athena,* while the puzzle pieces fell into place.

"And you didn't think to tell the police any of this?" Pearly said.

Eldon, ever curious, started ambling over to the pier. Pearly waved him off.

"We didn't want to bother them people, just growing some pot back in the woods," Ralph said.

"We figured it'd be safer to wait 'til they was gone," Jack added. "They'll have to be out of there in a week or so, before the frost."

"You don't want to mess with them people," BB said. "They'd as soon kill you as stomp a bug."

"Stomp, like Carl Mueller was stomped?" Pearly said angrily. "I can't believe you got Sarah and Oliver into this mess, knowing what those guys were doing."

"If we don't bother the pot farmers, they don't bother us," Ralph said. "We didn't think your friends would end up going after them people."

"We just wanted your friends to try and get the law off Ralph," Jack said.

"Besides, we don't know if them pot people killed Carl, anyhow," BB said. "Could have been somebody else, like whoever spiked that tree. All we wanted your friends to do was show that Ralph didn't kill anybody."

"Then Sarah started asking about them ATV trails," Ralph added, "and we figured she was headed for trouble."

"Anyways, now you know," Jack said, "and you can tell your friends to stop looking around, and maybe riling those guys up and gettin' themselves hurt."

"I can't believe you're telling me this," Pearly said in amazement. "Were you ever going to tell the cops?"

"Half the town knows what's going on back in there, and they haven't said anything, so why should we look for trouble?" Jack said.

Jack was right, Pearly thought. How many people around Tyler knew about the pot, but were too intimidated to say anything on the principle of "let sleeping dogs lie?" How many people just plain didn't care about a few pot plants in the woods?

"If the police was to arrest poor old Ralph, then we'd probably say something about them people," BB said, "if we thought it'd get him off."

"Do you know how much pot there is?" Pearly said.

"Hell," Jack replied, "It must be a good junk of the stuff. They're growing it outside instead if in doors, and they've got three guards watching it."

"No idea where it might be?" Pearly said.

"Wherever it is," Jack replied earnestly, "we ain't about to look, what with them guards around."

Chapter 30

S mall animals, and perhaps the crow they'd heard earlier, had been gnawing on Ken's face, but it was clearly his body tucked out of sight behind the fallen tree trunk.

Martha looked down at the corpse in silence.

"We need to call the police," Sarah said.

Martha didn't respond at first, then seemed to shake herself. "There's no cell phone coverage here. There's hardly any out on the paved road. Besides, if we did call the cops, they'd tell us to stay put so they could spend the rest of the day asking questions, like why we were here."

"What's wrong with that?"

"What's wrong is that I want to know what's at the back of the woodlot that Carl didn't have a chance to get to. And it'll be a lot easier without the cops around." Martha gave a last glance at Ken. "Besides, he's not going anywhere."

"Do you want to get yourself killed too? Let the police look, if you think there's something back there."

"Let the police look? They haven't come up with anything yet.

Besides, I have a gun."

"You know why Carl was killed, don't you?" Sarah said.

"I can make a guess," Martha replied. She turned away, consulted her GPS, and started off into the woods.

"And you know who killed him, too," Sarah said. "You knew the minute you saw this tree."

Martha stopped in her tracks, turned. "If you're so smart, who do *you* think killed Carl?"

"Obviously somebody who knew how to use a chainsaw."

Martha gave her a "duh" look. "That's most everyone around here, including me," she said.

"It had to be somebody who knew these woods and this clearing," Sarah added. "Another thing: there were two standing dead trees—this one and the spiked cedar. That had to mean something to the killer—something that you recognized just now."

Martha sighed, nodded.

"At first I thought that choosing dead trees was symbolic of something, a statement of some kind," Sarah went on, thinking out loud, "but now I think it was simpler than that. I think whoever did this instinctively selected dead trees for his purposes, rather than damaging living trees unnecessarily."

"Someone who spends his life deciding which tree will live and which will die, for the greater good," Martha added.

"Dan Finlon."

"At first I thought Bruce Nash was behind it," Martha said, "trying to get SOCC out of the way so he could get on with his tree cutting. But why would he go to all the trouble of choosing dead trees? Alive or dead, they're just dollars on the stump to him."

"Knowing Dan is a killer doesn't answer the big question—the why," Sarah said. "And why tell the police where Carl's body was, when it would have been so easy to hide?"

"The only way to answer all that is to finish the job Carl started,"

Martha replied, "and that's what I'm going to do."

"Leave it to the police," Sarah pleaded. "Two people have been killed already."

"You can stay here if you want, but it's more than a mile through the woods to the back corner that Carl never got to, and I want to be home by afternoon, so I'm taking off now," Martha said.

"Do whatever you want," Sarah replied, "but I'm going out to the road and call 911." Just then, a sudden noise made her turn.

"Toss the cell phone over here," Dan said as he entered the clearing, a gun in his hand. "Yours too, Kirkland. And that GPS unit in your hand."

They did as they were told.

"I figured this would be a good place to look for you two," he said as he ground their cells under his heel.

"Hey, that's a brand new phone," Sarah protested.

"So you really did kill him," Martha said, her voice flat. Sarah saw no tears in her companion's eyes now, only fury and hatred.

"And Ken, too, I suppose," Sarah added.

"I was hoping the cops would have found Ken by now," Dan replied. "Guess I'll have to tip them off when we're done here. With luck, they'll hold up Nash's woodcutting for a couple more days."

"What difference does that make?" Sarah said.

Dan shrugged instead of answering, kicked the ruined phones away, and glanced at the GPS. "Good thing I found you."

"You didn't have to kill anybody," Martha said, softly.

Dan sighed. "I wouldn't have if he'd minded his own business instead trespassing on private property, hunting for his precious cedars, the damn tree-hugging fool. So, I gave him a tree to hug."

Martha sagged, head drooping, heaving great sobs.

"Why did you shoot up SOCC headquarters?" Sarah said, hoping to distract Dan from Martha.

"Isn't it obvious?" Dan replied. "To make people think Bruce

Nash was getting back at them for burning his harvester, and to encourage them to keep on picketing."

Sarah thought about Oliver's conjurer. "Which you burned yourself, to stir up more trouble. It was all to stir up trouble."

"You're not as dumb as I thought." Dan turned to Martha. "Jesus, Kirkland, get it together. We haven't got all day," he said. "I don't want to shoot you two, and clutter this place up with more bodies.

He tensed as Martha fumbled in her jeans pocket.

"Martha—" Sarah warned.

It was only a handkerchief. Martha wiped her eyes, blew her nose loudly, slipped the handkerchief back into her pocket.

It was a magician's trick.

The little pistol was almost invisible in Martha's hand as she suddenly straightened up.

Sarah's warning shout, four quick, whiplash shots, the heavy report of Dan's Glock, Martha and Dan falling, then silence descended on the clearing.

———

"What the hell do you think you're doing?" Pearly demanded. He and Eldon had found Oliver bending over his sawmill.

"Taking the blade off the mill so I can get it trued up. That log of yours put a warp in it," Oliver replied.

"In your condition?"

"My condition is fine. It's the blade that's warped."

"You're both warped," Pearly retorted. "You're barely out of the hospital, for one thing—"

"Two days isn't 'barely.'"

"—and I bet that saw blade weighs more than you're supposed to lift," Pearly concluded, nodding to Eldon.

The young man extracted the wrench from Oliver's hand.

"It's a left-handed thread on the nut," Oliver said to Eldon.

"Yeah, yeah," Eldon replied.

"We came up to let you know why Ralph fired you and Sarah," Pearly said while Eldon went to work on the saw blade's oversized retaining nut.

"You talked to him?"

"The whole crew caught up with me earlier this morning," Pearly replied. "Apparently, they think there's a mess of pot planted up in the back of Denton's woodlot, and they were afraid you and Sarah might get hurt if you stumbled over it."

"You've got to be kidding," Oliver said in exasperation. "Why the hell didn't they say something before?"

Pearly shrugged. "Said they didn't want to stir up a ruckus."

"See no evil," Oliver muttered.

"There are some tough guys guarding the pot, according to Jack," Pearly said.

Eldon had managed to remove the nut and was looking cautiously at the saw teeth. Oliver nodded at a pair of heavily padded leather gloves lying on the brow of the mill.

"Too small," Eldon said, ambling off. "I got a pair in the truck."

"My guess is that Carl was wandering around in there looking for cedars to save, got too close to the pot plantation, and got killed for his trouble," Pearly said.

Okay, but why tell the cops where Carl's body was?" Oliver said. "And why shoot up SOCC, or wreck Briskin's pulp truck? Or all the other things?"

"You're the detective," Pearly grumbled, "you tell me."

Eldon returned with his oversized gloves and removed the saw blade as though it was little more than a dinner plate.

"I'll pay to have it hammered," Pearly said. "Put it in your truck," he told Eldon.

"No need for you to pay," Oliver replied.

"It was my tree that wrecked it," Pearly countered. "I feel bad about that."

"So what do the spikes have to do with the pot farm?" Pearly inquired as Eldon carried his giant dinner plate away.

"Good question," Oliver replied. "We're missing something, but I don't know what."

"Where's Sarah?" Eldon said, returning.

"She went to Augusta to do some shopping. Something about buying stuff for the cabin she's renting," Oliver replied. "She'll be back later this afternoon."

"The Rankin cabin," Pearly said to Eldon.

"I thought that place was furnished," Eldon said. "And what's wrong with shopping in Rockland? "It's a hell of a lot closer than Augusta."

"You'll understand certain things about women and shopping when you get married," Pearly informed his young employee.

The three men looked at each other for a second.

"God damn!" Oliver exclaimed. "She was talking to Martha what's-her-name, the vice president of SOCC, at yesterday's riot."

"What's Sarah's number?" Pearly said.

"I've got it in the house," Oliver replied.

"I've got it here," Eldon said, retrieving a battered cell phone from his belt.

"Did it ever occur to you, Ollie," Pearly said, "that your life would be a lot better if you had a cell?"

Oliver frowned. He didn't like the nickname, which was why Pearly used it. "I've had a bad experience with cell phones," he muttered.

"Just because your last cell exploded doesn't mean they *all* blow up, for crissakes," Pearly retorted.

"She doesn't answer," Eldon said. "It goes right to voice mail."

"Maybe it's not working," Pearly suggested.

"It's brand new," Oliver replied. "She just got it to replace the one that was stolen."

"Probably doesn't mean anything," Pearly said.

"Maybe she turned it off," Eldon suggested.

"Or maybe she's in a place where there's no coverage," Oliver countered.

"It'll take us a good hour to get there," Pearly said.

"Might as well take my truck," Eldon said.

"Get his gun," Martha said between gritted teeth as Sarah leaned over her.

"I'm taking care of you first. I don't think he'll be needing it, and I have to stop the bleeding."

"I'm fine," Martha insisted with an involuntary groan of pain. "Just get the goddamn gun!"

"The man is dead, Martha! I checked, and he's full of bullet holes!" Sarah screeched. She caught herself, went on more calmly. "I don't see the gun, anyway—it must have flown out of his hand when he fell. And I'm not going to waste time looking for it until your leg is bandaged up." Sarah was using her pocket knife to cut up a spare sweatshirt which she'd found in the bottom of Martha's backpack.

"Are you *sure* he's dead? What if he isn't? What if he's playing possum? You've got to find the gun!"

"I am a nurse, Kirkland," Sarah retorted emphatically, "and if I say somebody is dead, that person is D.E.A.D. God, you're the stubbornest woman I've ever met."

Martha groaned as Sarah wrapped her makeshift dressing around

Martha's bloody jeans.

"You're also the luckiest woman I've ever met," Sarah added. "If that bullet had hit a bone, you wouldn't have a leg left for me to bandage, and if it had hit an artery, you wouldn't have any blood left for me to sop up."

"We have to get out of here," Martha said, the near-hysteria gone. "He won't be alone."

"I'll run out to the main road and call 911 as soon as I'm done with this. He may have wrecked our cells, but there must be a phone on him somewhere."

They heard voices, the crackle of brush in the distance.

"Too late for that," Martha muttered.

There were times when talking to Tony Demano made Sal's thumbs feel prickly, and this was one of those occasions.

"How are things with you, Salvatore?" Tony asked, adopting his usual the-phone-is-bugged style.

"Busier than hell," Sal replied, meaning that things were getting out of control.

"A man shouldn't overwork himself," The Thumb said in his paternal voice. "I worry about you getting too tired. I'm worried about our associate, too. I'm not sure he's going to work out for us." Sal figured Tony wasn't asking about Vinnie.

"He's pretty busy right now, Uncle Tony, but I think he'll be okay once business slows down. All the damn end-of-the-season tourists keep everybody hopping."

There was a moment of silence while Tony deciphered Sal's words.

"What about that conservation group you're working with?" Tony said, going down his worry list like a helicopter parent. "Is the new head guy doing okay?"

"He's under a lot of pressure from some of the members," Sal replied, thinking about Martha. "And he's still grieving over Carl."

"Too much grief is a bad thing," Tony commented. "Talk to him. Help him to forget about the past and move on."

Sal realized that he hadn't seen Ken since yesterday on the picket line. His thumbs really began to tingle now. "I'll talk to him this afternoon," Sal promised.

———

Sarah admired Martha's determination. In what must be excruciating pain, and with her arm over Sarah's shoulder for support, they were making remarkably good progress through the woods.

Even so, they were still close enough to hear the murmur of voices in the clearing behind them.

It wouldn't be long before Dan's thugs took in the situation, realized their quarry was somewhere near, and spotted the tracks.

"Pick up the pace," Martha hissed between clenched teeth.

"You may not mind sprinting through the woods with your leg half shot off," Sarah panted, "but I'm getting tired."

"Would you rather be tired or dead?"

"Somebody must have heard the shots and called the cops," Sarah said hopefully as they labored on.

"You sure are a city girl, Cassidy." Martha's words were coming a few at a time as though each one was a painful struggle. "It's miles to the nearest house, and with Nash's machinery running, nobody would hear the shots, anyway. Besides, this is the country. People shoot guns around here all the time. Nobody pays attention."

They struggled on, Martha's arm getting heavier and heavier on Sarah's shoulder as Martha hopped along, urging a faster pace. The woods were thick here, filled with second-growth trees and brush—good for concealment, bad for speed.

"I don't feel so good," Martha muttered, sagging against Sarah.

Sarah eased her to the ground in a tiny open spot. Martha looked ashen, her face cold and sweaty. Worse, her jeans were soaked with blood, leaving a trail of red on the leaves behind them.

"This may hurt," Sarah said, "but I need to retie the bandage tighter."

"What the hell kind of a nurse were you?" Martha said, gritting her teeth while Sarah worked.

Sarah took off her windbreaker, using its sleeves and Martha's belt to tie it in place.

"Hurry it up," Martha hissed. "I can hear our friends back there. And make sure you stop the bleeding or we'll never lose those guys. We must be leaving a hell of a blood trail."

"We've got to hide, Martha. We'll never make it out to the main road like this before they catch up with us, and they're between us and the logging road."

"So we hide. Then what?"

"We can hold them off with your gun until somebody comes along. They won't dare to hang around forever."

"Too bad you didn't bother to get his gun," Martha grumbled.

"I didn't have much time, remember?"

"Leave me here, and run for help," Martha said. "There's no reason for them to get both of us."

"Not going to happen. I'll carry you."

"Are you nuts? You're a city girl and I've got a good fifteen pounds on you," Martha said. They could hear voices closing in behind them.

Sarah knew they had only one chance. She looked into Martha's glassy eyes. "Isn't that old cellar hole right around here?"

Martha struggled to focus. "Yes. Think I can find it."

They pushed on through the heavy brush with Sarah carrying

Martha fireman-style.

"Bear more to the left, thicker brush," Martha murmured after a while. "How many times did I shoot that bastard?"

"Four," Sarah gasped. She figured that Martha had grossly understated their weight difference.

"One shot left, then."

"You only have one shot left?"

"The revolver only had five bullets in it. Safer to carry that way. Jesus, Cassidy, if I'd known we were going to fight off an army of goons, I'd have packed an Uzi."

"At least they don't know how many shots we have left."

"They'll find out soon enough," Martha grumbled. "Bear to the right, and or chrissake stop tramping so hard on the brush. You want to lead them right to us?"

"You are a pain in the butt, Kirkland. If you didn't weigh so much, I wouldn't have to tramp so hard."

Before long, they came to a spot where brush was thinner, and Sarah caught a glimpse of the huge lilac bush.

"We're here," she said. "I'll be damn glad to get you off my back."

There was no reply from Martha.

Chapter 32

"Dan is dead?" Sal said, his hands sweaty on the cell, his mind churning with apprehension.

"We found him in . . . clearing. One of the . . . must . . . shot him," one of the guards replied, the words coming between bursts of static.

"You're breaking up," Sal said. "Don't forget you're working for Tony Demano and me now, with Dan dead."

"Don't worry. . . still after them."

"Did you say you have them?"

"Not yet, but. . . closing in. I'm out on the road. . . keep them away from their car. . . must have winged one. . . Lots of blood—"

"Lots of blood?" Sal interrupted.

". . . can't go much further. One of them's got. . . in bad shape."

"Can you see them?"

"No. It's. . . brush in there, can't see. . . fifty feet."

"Have they had time to call for help?"

"Don't think so. We got. . . right after the shots . . . pushing them pretty hard."

More and more, Sal was beginning to wish he was back in some backwater shopping mall, boosting cars. "I want them, before anybody else finds them."

"Five minutes, tops. . .they're going slower. . .we'll. . .them surrounded. . ."

"Call me when you've got them," Sal said urgently.

Sal put the broke the tenuous connection, and called Vinnie's cell, praying that his headstrong assistant could be reached.

Vinnie picked up on the first ring.

"Jeez," Vinnie said after Sal had filled him in. "Do you think the broads know what's going on?"

"They know Ken is dead," Sal said. "Plus, one of them shot Dan. Tony is going to be pissed."

"I thought getting Finlon out of the way was part of Tony's plan," Vinnie said.

"Killing him wasn't what Tony had in mind, you idiot. Especially not now," Sal growled. "The cops will go ape-shit if they find four more bodies up there, assuming Dan's guys get Cassidy and Kirkland."

"Yeah," Vinnie replied, chastened, "I guess that is kind of overdoing it."

"Damn right it is. Dan and I had planned to dump the broads behind SOCC headquarters in Augusta to keep the cops guessing. A couple of bodies up there in the boonies is bad enough, but if the cops decide there's a serial killer on the loose, they'll turn that woodlot inside out." Sal though for a moment. "I want you to go and watch Martha's car, in case something else goes wrong."

"I won't be able to reach you on my cell from there," Vinnie replied.

"Doesn't matter. I want somebody with brains right on the spot to tell Dan's goons what to do, now he's dead. I don't want any more bodies cluttering up those woods."

———————

Eldon's truck rumbled through Brooks on its way north.

"You guys want to pick up a few subs at the store here?" Eldon said hopefully.

"Keep it rolling," Pearly replied.

"I still think this is a wild goose chase," Eldon muttered.

"She's still not answering her cell," Pearly pointed out.

"Doesn't prove she's up there in the woods," Eldon said. "There's lots of places that don't have coverage."

"In Augusta?" Pearly said.

"Maybe she turned it off so she would be distracted while she shopped," Eldon suggested.

Oliver, who had been sitting in silence, spoke up. "There's something more about all the things that have been happening. It's a series of distractions all right, but they're more than that. They're also a series of delaying tactics. Carl's murder, trashing the timber harvester, wrecking Briskin's pulp truck, all of SOCC's picketing, have one thing in common: they all delayed Nash's timber cutting." Oliver paused. "Okay, the way Carl was murdered was some kind of a statement, but it also slowed Nash down, what with all the police investigations."

"Which means the pot farm is probably somewhere near where he'll be cutting soon," Pearly said.

"But not too near, or the police would have found it," Oliver said.

"And the pot farmers want to slow things down until the weed is ripe and they can they harvest it," Eldon added.

"After the plants have bloomed, according to Jack," Pearly said. "Which can't be all that long."

"Jack, the pot expert," Oliver mused.

Gasping for breath and staggering under Martha's dead weight, Sarah stared into the darkness of the cellar hole.

The cellar hole seemed to be staring back.

Martha, still unconscious, stirred and the motion nearly toppled Sarah into the abyss. She lurched back from the edge, irrational fear of what lay in front of her fighting with the very real threat of her pursuers. She lay Martha on the ground and stooped over her for a moment, panting, working up the courage to enter the gloom, realizing that she had no other choice.

Martha's dead weight made it a lot harder to get her into the cellar hole, but the collection of leaves and twigs that covered the ground made a soft place for her to lie on.

It felt like a different world down here. The noises of birdsong and of pursuit were muffled to inaudibility, leaving an eerie and somehow disturbing stillness—except for the frantic beating of her heart.

A jungle of overhanging foliage kept the space in a damp, cool perpetual darkness. A darkness where the spirits of generations of Dentons seemed to live on.

Spirits who did not welcome the new arrivals.

"Martha, wake up," Sarah said urgently, with a shake.

"Bury me," Martha muttered faintly.

"I'm the nurse, and I'll tell you when you're dead, dammit," Sarah snapped. Her eyes were gradually adjusting to the dark and she could see Martha's face rallying.

"For crying out loud, I have no intention of dying, Cassidy," Martha replied, her voice stronger. "I just want you to bury me under the leaves. Less likely to see me if they look in here. Warmer too."

Martha groaned as she shifted to pull the revolver from her jeans pocket. "You may need this when you go for help. Now start shoveling those leaves."

Sarah checked Martha's makeshift bandage first. "I can't be sure in the dark, but as near as I can tell the bleeding looks like it's pretty much stopped," she said. "Probably because you're lying still."

"I'm not planning to go anywhere."

Sarah began scooping armloads of leaves over Martha until only her face was visible. That done, she ran her hands over the rest of area to smooth out the disturbed places. A sudden pain stabbed her right hand and she snatched it away, feeling more than seeing the warmth of blood running across her palm.

Something glistened in the shadows. Gingerly, she picked it up, a stainless steel steak knife, its surface unmarred after sixty years of lying in the moldy duff. The handle was damaged by fire and age, but the serrated blade felt sharp as new.

"Time for you to get going," Martha said. "Waiting here until dark is too dangerous. Besides, I may not last that long," Martha added in a matter-of-fact voice. "You've got to get out of here now and get help."

Sarah knew that Martha was right, but the idea of leaving her behind. . .

"Are you going to deny the last request of a dying woman?" Martha said.

"You are one ornery bitch," Sarah grumbled.

"Never forget it."

"You keep the gun," Sarah told Martha. "It only has one shot in it anyway, and I've got this," she said holding the steak knife. "That way, if one of those guys sees you, you can tell him you've got an Uzi and put a bullet in his head."

Sarah tucked Martha's backpack under the leaves. You've got energy bars and plenty of water in there. Stay hydrated."

"Yes, nurse," Martha replied. "And make sure you've got my car keys."

Before she got up, Sarah glared into the dark corners of the cellar and sternly warned the spirits to take good care of Martha Kirkland, or she would come back and carve them up with their own steak knife.

It was her over-stressed imagination, of course—there were no spirits—but Sarah seemed to feel them cringe before her.

"You're not as bad a person as I thought at first, Cassidy," Martha said as Sarah turned to leave.

"Neither are you," Sarah replied.

"It's too bad you're so damn stubborn," they said in unison.

Chapter 33

S arah stood at the edge of the cellar hole for several minutes looking for some sign of their pursuers. Strangely, she now felt reluctant to leave what had become her refuge.

"Are you going to stand there all afternoon?" Martha said after a while. "Pull yourself together and get going before I take a shot at you."

Sarah turned to the shadows where Martha lay. "You brought the gun along because you were hoping to find Carl's killer. You were planning to hunt him down, weren't you?"

"Get your buns in gear, Cassidy, and try not to sound like an elephant going through the woods."

"Shut up and save your strength."

"I'll be pissed if you aren't back in time for my supper. Do you know how to get to the road from here?"

"Yes," Sarah replied, crawling slowly up and out of the cellar. She had tucked the knife in her belt at the small of her back. She checked that it was still there.

Sarah darted across a patch of open ground, heading for the

thick, brushy woods of the old hay fields. No shouts or gunshots greeted her.

It wasn't far to the road from here, where Martha's car and safety waited. Sarah moved as quickly as she dared, while trying not to sound like Martha's proverbial elephant. The temptation to make a mad dash for it, cover the last few hundred yards as quickly as possible, was almost irresistible, but some of Dan's henchmen were almost certainly between her and the road.

Sarah was so focused on moving quietly that didn't even notice the man until he stepped out from behind a tree and grabbed her left arm in a bone-crushing grip.

"I've got one!" he yelled, jerking Sarah off her feet.

She struggled to regain her footing, her right hand reaching instinctively for the knife in her belt—a sweeping slash across his arm. The knife cut through his jacket like butter, the serrated blade sawed into bone. God, this thing is sharp, she thought as she felt him let go of her, bellowing in pain.

She spun away, caught a glimpse of him doubled over, clutching his arm, blood spurting between his fingers.

No point in stealth now. Sarah ran headlong for the road, less than a hundred yards away.

A fist caught the side of her head, staggered her back against a tree. The fist's owner swore, shaking his bruised hand, then charged at her, readying another blow. Dazed, ears ringing, she half jumped, half fell against him as he swung at her, drove the knife into his side, slashed at his leg as she fell.

There was no more pursuit.

Sarah stumbled, breathless, out of the woods, only fifty feet from Martha's Prius. It was easy now. Find somebody who could call for help, maybe one of Nash's men, and it would be over.

Sarah collapsed against the car door, gasping for breath, head still ringing from the last goon's blow, the bloody knife still clutched in her hand. After a moment, she put the knife back in her belt and was fishing the keys out of her pocket when a car pulled up behind her and Vinnie got out.

"I've been driving up and down this road for an hour waiting for you to turn up." he grumbled. There was a gun in his hand.

Sarah looked at him, her heart sinking. A few more seconds and she would have been safely away. "Martha has been shot. She needs a doctor, or she'll die," she said, knowing her words were a waste of time.

Vinnie looked at the woods nervously. "Why don't you show me where she is, and I'll call 911?"

"Call 911 first. She needs help now."

"Not going to happen, Cassidy," he said. "What you and I are going to do is take a ride in Martha's little go-cart. Let's go, before somebody comes along."

"You drive," he added, waving her towards the car with his gun, "and I'll give directions."

"I don't imagine you will," came a voice from the edge of the woods.

Sarah turned to see Ralph clambering out of the woods and onto the road, a double barreled shotgun at the ready.

"Get the hell out of here gramps," Vinnie snarled.

"Put that gun down or I'll put the lead to you quicker'n spit."

Vinnie gazed at the twin 12-gage barrels lined up on his chest. "This is none of your business, old man. Go home," he blustered.

"Two loads of double-aught buckshot is goin' to make a helluva mess of you at this distance," Ralph commented. "I was you, I'd put the pistol down and toss me your car keys."

Vinnie, his eyes fixed venomously on Ralph's shotgun, put his gun down. "You're in a hell of a lot of trouble, pops," he growled.

"Can't argue that," Ralph said with a sigh. "Now start walking down the road."

"You all right?" Ralph said to Sarah, as soon as Vinnie was well away. He tossed Vinnie's keys into the woods and picked up the automatic.

"I am now," she replied. "Thank God you came along. We need to call 911. Martha's been shot."

Ralph reached slowly for the cell clipped to his belt. And stopped, seemingly lost in thought.

"She needs help *now!*" Sarah struggled with her composure.

"Best we get in the car first, drive down the road a ways in case there's any more of those guys in the woods," Ralph said. "You better drive."

Sarah had forgotten about the goons. There must still be one more around somewhere. She wasted no time getting into the car while Ralph eased into the passenger seat, slipping his shotgun into the back.

"Why don't you call 911 while we drive?" she suggested, her patience way past running thin.

"Time for that later," Ralph replied vaguely.

"Don't you understand? She may be dead later!"

"Can't call, cell's dead out here," he replied.

"Can you at least try?" Sarah looked at Ralph, saw his expression, saw Vinnie's pistol in his hand, pointed at her side.

"I'll tell you where to turn," he said.

"Where are we going, anyhow?" Eldon asked.

"We're going to find Sarah and Martha," Oliver said.

"And how are you going to do that when you don't know where they are?" Pearly said impatiently.

"I'm betting that Ralph has a good idea, and I'm going to get it out of him," Oliver replied grimly.

"And I suppose you think Ralph killed Carl Mueller, after all," Pearly said disgustedly. "The man is as honest as the day is long."

"That's the trouble; I think he's too honest," Oliver replied, "and it's gotten him into trouble."

_____

Chapter 34

Eldon lurched his truck to a stop in Ralph's crowded dooryard. They could see a face appear briefly at the kitchen window.

"Lot of people in there," Eldon commented, indicating the assorted vehicles. "What do we do now? Call the cops?"

"No time," Oliver said, a sense of urgency spurring him on. "Besides, I think we'll get more out of Ralph without the police."

"Ralph isn't the only person in there," Pearly warned as Oliver got out and headed for the door.

_____

The kitchen was crowded even before Oliver, Pearly, and Eldon entered. Ralph, with Sarah to his left, was seated at the table with their backs to the door. To Sarah's left was an older woman, who Oliver took to be Ralph's wife, Irma. Two younger men, looking to be in their twenties, sat across the table, facing the door and looking aggressively at the new arrivals.

There were guns everywhere Oliver looked.

Sarah started to get up, but Ralph restrained her with his left hand, gesturing with the blocky-looking automatic in his right fist—a Glock, Oliver guessed.

"Your grandsons, the pot farmers, I suppose," Oliver said, looking at the two young men. He turned to Ralph. "That's why you were lying to us. You were trying to protect your grandsons. Irma didn't move out because of the picketing, did she? I'm guessing that she left because the two of you disagreed about your grandsons' pot growing."

"Our lives ain't any of your business," Irma growled. "Ralph told you to go and leave us in peace, but you people just can't let things be."

"I hope you've settled your differences," Oliver replied.

Irma glared.

"Didn't take you long to get here," Ralph said in a resigned, defeated voice.

"I want you out of my house right now," Irma said, reaching for the double barreled shotgun propped against the table beside her.

"You got a lot of nerve kidnaping Sarah, and we're not leaving without her," Eldon retorted. Though he stood behind his companions, Eldon's height and girth made him a looming presence. He moved forward, herding Oliver and Pearly before him into the room.

"Nobody kidnaped anyone," Ralph said, motioning his wife down. "Irma and me just wanted Sarah to see who she was about to put the law on."

"So she's seen us," one of the young men grumbled. "Can we go now?"

"You'll go when I tell you to," Ralph said to them. He turned to Oliver. "They didn't mean for anybody to get hurt, and that's why Farley and Finley found me when they learned that Dan was going to have those three guards of his do in Sarah and Martha. I went down to look for them myself, keep them from being killed, but

Sarah was out on the road 'bout the time I got there."

"So you forced her to come here?" Eldon said.

"I couldn't have her call the police," Ralph said dully. "They're good boys, just not so bright."

"All they wanted was to make enough to live on," Irma added. "A few wizeny plants—"

"There must be a thousand plants in there, Grandma," Farley said, offended. "We put a ton of work into that field."

"I don't care how many plants there are!" Sarah exploded as she rose out of her chair, managing to elude Ralph's grasp. "All I care about is getting help for Martha! It's been almost two hours! She could have bled to death by now, if Dan's goons haven't found her first!"

"You don't need to worry about them guys," Ralph replied. "The third one was taking the two you cut up off to the hospital, last I saw."

"Does your friend care about the law?" Irma said coldly.

Sarah stopped short, thought about Martha—stubborn, opinionated, outspoken, idealistic Martha. Would her principles let her turn a blind eye on Farley, Finley, and their role in all this?

"I can't speak for Martha," Sarah replied slowly. "All I know is that if you let her die out there, it will be your doing. Not Dan's doing, or his goons doing, or even the Boston mobsters Dan wholesales your pot to. *You* will have killed her."

The room went still, and Sarah took a half-step from the table, her back brushing against Oliver. He rested his hand lightly on her shoulder. It was trembling, whether from cold or nerves he couldn't tell.

"She's right, mother," Ralph said in a low voice. He stared sadly at his grandsons, who seemed oblivious to the tension filling the room.

"There's right, and there's *right*," Irma retorted, "and taking care of your own blood and bone is what comes first. Those SOCC do-gooders don't mean nothing to me. They live in their fancy houses, and feel good about it when they put the law on those that grow what they smoke. If your friend hadn't been nosing round in the woods she wouldn't have gotten hurt, so that's on her, not us."

"Why don't we just straighten this problem out," Eldon said reasonably. "Where is she, anyhow?" he asked Sarah.

"Remember when we were up there the first time, and I started feeling funny?" Sarah said.

"Yeah." Eldon reached for his cell and found himself staring down the barrels of Irma's shotgun.

"Jeez, Louise," he grumbled, "this ain't getting us anywhere."

"Eldon is right," Oliver said, studying Ralph's face. "We can't just stand here. Martha may have figured out that there's a bunch of pot up there somewhere—and she's probably not the only one. But she doesn't know your grandsons are involved, so they're safe even if she does call the police."

"Hey," Farley said in alarm, "we put a ton of work into that field."

"They ain't never going to find it from the air," Finley added defiantly. "There's netting over it, and we spread the plants out all around under the trees. Dan showed us how to do all that."

"He did a lot more than that," Sarah said. "He killed Carl and Ken to keep them from finding your pot farm."

Ralph stared down at the table top, while Finley and Farley looked wide-eyed at Sarah.

"We didn't know nothing about Ken," Farley said. "We figured Carl got killed for threatening to make trouble for Bruce Nash."

"That's what Dan wanted everyone to think," Sarah said.

"He was stirring up trouble to protect your pot," Oliver added, "and to delay Bruce's cutting until after your harvest was in. He spiked the tree so Bruce would have to take the time to check the logs with a metal detector. He warned young Derwin about it, but he also knew I'd find the spikes when I sawed the logs. In between the tree spiking and police investigations, he must have slowed things down by at least a week so far."

"Dan shot up SOCC headquarters and sabotaged Pastor Briskin for the same reason," Sarah added, "to keep people stirred up, encourage more picketing and confrontation in order to delay Bruce."

"Dan was taking his sweet time goin' around in there," Ralph muttered, "and he knew about my spare saw from when he was working on the lot we're cutting."

"The point is," Oliver went on, turning to Irma, "that you can't keep your grandsons' pot secret any more, and keeping us hostage isn't going to help."

"It's all over," Sarah added. "Too many people—too many outsiders—know about the field to keep it a secret any more. And three people have died, so far—"

"Three people?" Ralph looked at her, confused.

"Dan was killed this morning." Sarah saw no need to mention Martha's role in his death.

"I told you this would happen," Ralph groaned. "I told you from the start those people were bad. We should have put an end to it then."

"We didn't mean for anything like this to happen, Grandpa," Finley said earnestly. "We didn't know Dan would bring in those three tough-guys, and they just took over."

"We put in too many plants this spring, is all," Farley said, "and we needed somebody to sell the stuff to, and Dan said he'd take care of selling the pot. He's buying the stuff from people all over to send down to Boston."

"That'll learn you to get mixed up with people from away," Irma said. "Can't trust them an inch."

"But they're the ones with the money," Finley pointed out.

Oliver looked at Ralph's face, saw sadness, defeat. And something more. "Where are Jack and BB?" he asked Ralph quietly.

Ralph glanced reflexively at the fly-specked clock hanging on the wall. "I never wanted you two poking around in my business in the first place," he said. "It was Jack insisted on it, 'make you feel better,' he told me. Well, you've been nothing but a thorn in my boot, so the four of you can rescue your friend and get out of my house, and leave us in peace to take care of ourselves."

His eye on Irma's shotgun, Eldon opened his cell.

"We won't report Farley and Finley to the police," Sarah said reassuringly.

"Police couldn't prove anything anyhow," Ralph told her.

"What do you mean they couldn't prove anything, Grandpa? Our stuff is all over there," Farley said, a dawning horror on his face.

Ralph sighed, turned to Oliver. "Jack and BB must be done picking up by now."

"The first chance you've had when nobody was home?" Oliver murmured.

Ralph nodded and turned to Sarah. "Guess maybe you did some good after all, keeping those goons busy this afternoon."

"Grandpa!" Finley and Farley howled.

_____

Chapter 35

"**D**o you know why Indian Summer is my favorite time of year, Salvatore?" Tony The Thumb said.

"No, Uncle Tony," Sal replied nervously. "Why is that?" Sal had been twiddling his thumbs, so to speak, for almost a week while he waited in dread for this meeting.

"Because it reminds me of the summer, all the things that have happened. It's a time to evaluate; you know what I mean? It's a time think about what happened: what was good, and what wasn't so good."

There was no 300-dollar-a-bottle wine today. In fact, there was no restaurant, fancy or otherwise, either. Instead, they were sitting on a park bench on Boston Common, sharing a paper bag full of popcorn between themselves and a horde of pushy pigeons.

"Things didn't work out as I had hoped, Salvatore," Tony commented sadly.

Sal opened his mouth to list the various excuses he'd come up with, but Tony silenced him with a gesture.

"The police picked up two of Dan's guys who were guarding the crop," Tony went on. "They were cut up pretty bad. You used a burn phone when you talked to them?"

"Absolutely, Uncle Tony. There's no way they can be traced to us."

The Thumb nodded approvingly. "We've provided them with legal counsel—the best in the business—and they know the score, so you should be okay." Tony paused. "Still, I think you and Vinnie ought to lay low for a while. I have some work out in Lowell for the two of you."

"Yes, Uncle Tony," Sal replied, waiting for the other shoe to drop.

"I blame myself for this," Tony said. "I got carried away with this vertical integration idea, thought we could eliminate Dan Finlon—he was in so deep with his gambling debts—ease him out and end up working direct with the growers."

"SOCC was a perfect cover for that, Uncle Tony, and I was learning a lot about Dan's operation."

The Thumb nodded. "You're a quick study, Salvatore. The trouble is, we aren't farmers, we're business people, and we should stick with what we do best." The pigeons went into a frenzy as Tony flipped a handful of popcorn at them.

Sal listened in silence, hardly believing his good fortune. He'd expected to be groveling at The Thumb's feet, along with the pigeons, and here was Tony Demano apologizing to *him?*

"This is a learning experience for all of us," Tony went on. "So, what did *you* learn, Salvatore?"

"Don't trust those goddam Mainers," Sal babbled.

Tony raised an eyebrow.

Sal rushed on. "I mean, they don't think like us. You can't tell what they'll do next. Like Dan Finlon. The guy was a loose cannon."

"He was an Irishman," Tony commented.

Sal was startled by that. He supposed The Thumb's prejudice

must hark back a hundred years to the days when Italian immigrants settled in Boston's North End, while the Irish moved into the South End. The turf issues were bad enough, but when the Irish took over the police and got into politics—

"He was also kinda crazy," Sal added, "with all his tree hang-ups."

Tony nodded. "A good lesson. Know who you're working with." He gazed benignly at Sal. "You did good with Vinnie, taught him a lot."

"He's a smart kid, a quick learner," Sal replied.

"You two should work together for a while," Tony added pensively, "but not in Maine."

It had been a busy week, with Sarah getting ready to move into her cabin, and helping Oliver work on *Daisy*, which was now right-side up and ready to have her interior put in. With the spikes removed, she and Eldon had spent most of today helping Oliver saw Pearly's cedar logs into boards.

Oliver's hair and clothing were still sprinkled with sawdust, and he smelled like a cedar closet as he sat beside her on the sofa, the Defiant woodstove giving off a welcome heat.

"You didn't overdo it today, did you?" she asked, having noticed him grimace when he put an oversized piece of firewood into the stove.

"I'm fine. Better and better every day." He changed the subject, adding, "How is Martha, by the way?"

"I called her yesterday, and she's out of the hospital—for which the nursing staff is thankful, I'm sure—but she has months of physical therapy to go before she can walk without a limp. There was a lot of tissue damage."

"Is she okay with the police?"

"Why wouldn't she be? She shot him in self-defense. He fired first."

Oliver looked at her solemnly. The bruise on her head had turned a strange greenish color. "Is that what Martha told them?"

"She was too confused to remember clearly; it happened so fast. Anyway, that's what *I* told them." Sarah paused. "I'm not sure they believed me."

"Probably because of the four bullets in Dan's body."

"I never knew anybody could shoot that fast," she said.

"Adrenalin can do that. She's going to be running SOCC now?"

"Yes, though things will be tight without Sal bankrolling them."

"She'll probably end up saving more cedars with fewer picket lines."

They sat for a while and let the stove's heat flow over them, while Wes snored contentedly at their feet.

"Did you know what Ralph was up to all along?" Sarah said at last.

"You mean about him keeping us in his kitchen while Jack and BB cleaned up any trace of Finley and Farley from the pot farm?"

Sarah nodded.

"It dawned on me while we were sitting there that, with Dan and the guards out searching for you and Martha, and the grandsons in the kitchen, there wasn't anybody to watch the farm—probably the first chance Ralph had to put an end to it all without getting his grandsons in trouble."

"What did Jack and BB find up there?"

"Jack figured that Farley and Finley's marijuana plants were scattered over fifteen acres or so to make them less conspicuous, but of course, Jack was mostly interested in picking up the campsite there to get rid of the evidence."

Sarah nodded. "The whole thing made the front page of the

Bangor Daily News," she said, picking up the paper. "'Anonymous tip leads to marijuana farm in the Maine woods. Dan Finlon, a local forester, is linked to out-of-state mobsters in illicit drug operation.' Apparently Dan was managing, if that's the right word, three other marijuana plantations in the area, providing security, and working as a middleman between the growers and the mob."

"He was in a good position to do that," Oliver commented. "Nobody would question a forester wandering around the woods, looking at trees. In fact, he wouldn't have had a problem with the Denton property at all if Young Denton hadn't been so impatient to have the woodlot cut off, and SOCC hadn't decided to get involved."

"Dan's life can't have been easy," Sarah mused. "That day he showed me around the woodlot, he seemed to really have a love of the trees—almost a kind of spiritual connection—and yet it was his job to help people cut them down. It must have been struggle reconcile that love with his profession."

"The paper said he was a compulsive gambler who owed his bookie a small fortune. Maybe gambling was his safety valve."

"Maybe," Sarah replied. "He probably got involved with the pot business to pay his gambling debts."

"And let's not forget Sal, Dan's partner in crime."

"Sal must have joined SOCC when Dan learned they were interested in Denton's woodlot."

"Protecting the mob's investment," Oliver added.

"He was able to keep SOCC away from the woodlot all summer, until Carl got too nosy. Then he changed tactics and used Carl's death as an excuse to picket the woodlot in order to help slow down the logging and distract SOCC from doing more prowling in Denton's woods."

"Better to picket than to prowl, as Ken learned the hard way."

Sarah got up and put another log in the stove. "I gather that nobody in town ratted out Finley and Farley."

"Why would they turn in their own neighbors, when there's somebody from away to blame instead?"

Sarah's steak knife was lying on the end table beside the sofa. Oliver picked it up. "The handle is pretty beat up," he commented.

"Yes, but it's still plenty sharp."

"Good quality stainless steel. Are you going to keep it?"

"Yes," she replied. "It's silly, but I can't help feeling that the knife was given to me. It certainly saved my life."

"That cellar hole saved both your lives," he said. "Maybe they're not so bad after all."

"There's always more than one way to look at something, even a cellar hole. Sometimes when you look at it, a cellar hole turns out to be just a cellar hole, and sometimes not. I'm still keeping the knife, though."

Sarah snuggled against Oliver's side, her head on his shoulder. "It's too bad your still an invalid," she murmured after a while, placing her hand on his thigh.

But Oliver was asleep.